SIT DOWN SHUT UP AND PULL THE TRIGGER

SIT DOWN SHUT UP AND PULL THE TRIGGER

PROTECTED BY THE DAMNED, BOOK 4

MICHAEL TODD

DISRUPTIVE IMAGINATION

To Family, Friends and
Those Who Love
to Read.
May We All Enjoy Grace
to Live the Life We Are
Called.

The creature's head almost rubbed the ceiling. Its claws flexed in agitation as it wandered back and forth in T'Chezz's office, which was situated between the flowing lava and the pile of tortured bodies.

T'Chezz's realm was unknown to man, but man was not unknown to *him*.

He had a plan; a plan that would destroy humanity at its core. But what he *hadn't* expected was Korbin and his team of Killers, and the other teams T'Chezz had been fighting all over the world.

He'd win in two areas, then a major setback would come at the hands of the demon hunters. It was becoming difficult for T'Chezz to keep all the balls in the air simultaneously, so he was going to have to focus.

His eyes narrowed. T'Chezz had thought the invasion would be seamless and entertaining, but as Barro stood in front of him for the second time, he realized that he might have underestimated the power these Damned wielded on Earth.

T'Chezz plopped into the massive stone seat at the front of the room and tapped his claws against its carved arms. He stared at the demon, who was injured and obviously terrified of him.

T'Chezz could see that Barro had fought hard, and though he was livid that things weren't progressing, getting rid of him just yet would be a mistake. It was hard to find loyal demons, especially in a place like hell—even when he had spent so much energy, effort, and trouble to find his ass once Barro had been killed…again.

If he hadn't needed the information, Barro would have been lost.

"Tell me again how many there were?" T'Chezz asked calmly.

"At first there were two," the demon began. "The black man and the girl, but then two more came, some freshly Damned male and a priest."

T'Chezz rubbed his chin. "It seems as if they have formed some sort of group or gang that is hunting us specifically."

"There is something else," the demon said quietly. "The girl…her demon is familiar."

"Familiar? How so?" T'Chezz asked.

"It's your sister," Barro admitted, putting his head down.

"So she *has* been up to no good." T'Chezz chuckled, his laughter sounding like two chunks of basalt rubbing together. "But you're telling me that she is *helping* these Damned? That's too much for me to believe."

"I know, but it's true," the demon told him. "She gave the human powers like her own during the fight: strength, agility, and healing ability. She screamed questions at me when I was dying, wanting to know your plans."

"How could she help them?" T'Chezz growled. "I hate the bitch—don't get me wrong—and would love nothing more than to watch her be buried on one of hell's deepest levels, but I am aghast at the idea that she was fighting *against* us. Helping the human destroy us."

"She helped the human fight *me*," the demon corrected. "Talked shit to me during the process, too. Stood in the background as the human used the fucking cross to send me back to hell, though I am pretty sure they underestimated your ability to bring us back."

T'Chezz stood up. "You were lucky I caught you before you plummeted farther down, or you would be picking hell's core out of your teeth right now."

"Well the weapons they have are no joke," Barro told him. "And they hurt like a motherfucker."

"A special cross?" T'Chezz shook his head. "How in the world did those dimwitted creatures become capable of creating a material like this?"

"I don't know," the demon admitted, "but it burned right through me and ultimately ended me."

"And the Damned holding it was fine?"

"I would guess."

"Interesting," T'Chezz growled, looking across the hellish landscape. "It's been centuries; possibly over a thousand years since anything like this has been spoken about. There have been rumors but no evidence—until now."

"They have swords and knives as well." He groaned.

"My legs were cut to ribbons, and when I got slashed across the belly it felt like my body had been thrown into a volcano. It takes the wind out of you and drops you to your knees. If I had that reaction, I can only imagine what it would do to the smaller beasts out there."

"It doesn't instantly kill you, then?" T'Chezz asked.

"Not me, though I don't know what effect it would have on other demons," he answered. "But it took quite a bit for the metal to penetrate my skin. Quicker than bullets, but not immediate. Still, it hurts like a sonofabitch, which puts us at a disadvantage when we are trying to focus on crushing those humans' tiny little bones."

"There hasn't even been a whisper about a new weapon until now, and we have had our watchdogs out there searching," T'Chezz said angrily. "Even a thousand years ago when it surfaced for the first time, it was only two swords—two swords that I was told were completely taken care of, with no trace for the humans to find. Those swords forced us into the darkness for a long time, fearful of what might happen if they surfaced once again after the Battle of Intaglio. However, after centuries of hiding, starving, and needing entertainment from the human creatures we have started to emerge again. Slowly at first, but now it has become a movement. The last thing I need is to have this kind of challenge following us around topside."

"Do you think your sister had anything to do with it?" the demon asked.

"With the swords?" T'Chezz chuckled. "No, she is too stupid to understand something on that level. She is just a thorn in my side, nothing more. This human she has infected...*she* may be tough. She may be *different*, but she sure as hell can be taken out if necessary. She is human, with the frailty of a human's body, the misguided tempers, and the emotional attachment to their human lives. She can be broken, and in due time I will make sure that she is. For now, though, I have larger issues to take care of—like this weapons problem. I don't know who is behind this or where they got this knowledge or how many of these tools are out there, but I can promise I will find out."

He stared out at the writhing bodies in the fires.

"Oh, yes." He chuckled to himself, rubbing his hands together. "I *will* find them, and when I do it will be their end—their very unfortunate end." He started out of his office, one particular figure catching his attention. "Right now we can get back to business, because I am in the mood for torture."

Katie got up from the couch and stretched her arms high over her head, then straightened her t-shirt and yawned. She had just finished another episode of the soap opera, and though she felt like taking a nap, she had a meeting with the other owners of her company to attend.

She hoped they had some good news; that things were starting to shape up. She hadn't really paid attention for the last few days, since she was still trying to fully recover from the battle with the demon.

Katie made her way down to the conference room to the left of Korbin's office. When she arrived Korbin, Calvin, and Damian were already there, sitting around the table waiting for her. Damian smirked when she walked into the room yawning, a hand covering her mouth, and Korbin just shook his head. She smiled at Calvin, who was looking stronger and healthier every day, and took her seat.

Korbin chuckled. "Thank you so much for joining us."

"Hey, I'm the owner of the company. It's only right I nonchalantly stroll in late," she argued, before another yawn destroyed her chance of sounding important.

"You aren't Bruce Wayne," Korbin sniped.

"No, but that would be awesome," She nodded and sat down. "Sorry."

"Anyway," Korbin replied, shaking his head, "the weapons are starting to come along now. Joshua seems to have gotten his groove, and every time I turn around there is a new weapon on the table. Before much longer we are going to have a stockpile, which is obviously a good thing and a bad thing. What we need to figure out now is how to go to market with these weapons, but unfortunately this is not as simple as selling them on Amazon."

"They should create an Amazon for us." Katie smiled. "That would be awesome."

"We could trade demons with other teams." Calvin laughed.

Korbin sighed. "Can we at least attempt to stay on track here?"

"Yep." Katie nodded and pretended to zip her lips closed.

"Okay, as far as the weapons are concerned, we knew from the beginning that we couldn't hide them from the other teams forever," Korbin said. "That being said, we will need enough for every team, or we will be risking way too much."

"Okay." Katie leaned forward. "So what does that mean? How many teams are there, and how many weapons do we give to each team?"

"Well, I was thinking we start by giving three to each team. If they want more, that is when the business side of things kicks in," Korbin said. "There are seventeen teams, and every single one of them gets a weapons budget from the higher-ups. We do three free to show our solidarity in this war, then from there we negotiate. At three weapons per team we are looking at a minimum of fifty-one weapons, but I would say we'll probably need closer to eighty in order to keep all the team leads happy enough to keep our secret."

"I don't understand why they wouldn't," Katie replied. "They would rather risk not having the weapons at all than buy however many more they want?"

"They would risk having to get them from the government, since they would get them for free, rather than caring about our company or our livelihoods outside the team's work," Korbin corrected. "We are all fighting for a single cause, sure, but each team generally fights alone, so there tends to be a separation emotionally between them. They are already going to be jealous that we have the best and newest weapons, and some won't find that fair since we are not the busiest team—or at least we weren't until recently."

"That's a shame," Katie said. "That's going to cost a hell of a lot of money."

"True," Damian said. "But with our increased kill rate, we are making some serious money right now."

Katie nodded. "We are."

"On top of that, Mamacita has gotten all our suppliers to agree to very favorable prices," Damian said. "We are currently in the black—which is more than most new companies can say, especially since we currently have zero profit."

"That's nuts." Katie stifled another yawn. "Damn! Sorry. I mean it's awesome, don't get me wrong. I just had no idea that Mamacita was as badass as she is."

"Yeah." Damian shook his head to stave off a sympathy yawn. "She is hardnosed and business-savvy. She has been running that house a long time, and has never had an issue. I think that compared to some of the clients over there, this is a walk in the park for her. Those suppliers? They run with their tails between their legs when she's on the line. I listened to her the other day. She started out all sweet and kind, and when they thought they could fuck with her because she was a woman...oh man, they probably went home and called their mommas."

Katie laughed. "That's awesome. We should have had her from the beginning. Things would've started out a lot smoother for us."

"Yeah." Damian chuckled. "Not only did she straighten *us* out, but she went back and renegotiated the old contracts, because they had stolen from Joshua's ancestors. Nobody even asked her to do it, either."

"Good," Katie said. "I have to admit that I have noticed I have money again. Talk about exciting, when I open up my hidden spot and moths don't fly out."

"Yes, yes." Korbin rolled a finger in the air. "We are all impressed by Mamacita. Can we move on?"

Katie laughed. "Sheesh, Korbin, what flew up your behind today?"

"Nothing," he snapped. "I just have a million things to do beyond this meeting, that's all. The other teams want a conference call about LA, the higher-ups need reports, and we still have work to do on this company."

"All right," Katie said, putting her hands up in surrender. "What's the next order of business?"

Katie sat back in the chair and let Korbin run the meeting. In reality she should have been running it, but she knew she was inexperienced.

She also had been completely out of the day-to-day of the business since LA, and really didn't want to look like an idiot. She figured she could learn something from watching Korbin and Damian, and even Calvin, because they had more experience than she did.

She wanted the company to be a success, but when it came down to it, she didn't have the knowledge base she needed for the world she was living in to run the company the way it should be run.

She knew the other world—and how to market things —but not the secret world of demon slaying, the relationships, and apparently the fucking politics. She would get there eventually, but for the time being she would just sit back and let them work it.

They are pretty good at this shit, Pandora said.

Yeah. Katie scoffed. *Way better than me.*

You'll get there, Pandora replied.

Aw, motivation, Katie cooed.

I just meant you'll probably sell a blade or two before my brother rips your spine from your body, Pandora qualified.

Wow, Katie said. *That... I just... Wow.*

What? Just being honest, Pandora replied.

Yeah, keep that honesty to yourself for a while, okay? Katie replied. *I need to focus on this meeting.*

Meeting, shmeeting. Pandora scoffed. *Once those babies are on the market, you are going to be set for life. We can eat all the food we want, buy whatever we want, and do whatever we want.*

In case you hadn't noticed, I can't *do whatever I want*, Katie replied. *I hunt your people—that's what I do. It's that, death, or research, remember?*

Did I say "whatever?" I meant "whoever." But we are still a damn caged rat, Pandora grumped. *We could take them.*

Be quiet, Katie replied. *I'm too busy for this.*

Whatever, Pandora said, going quiet.

Katie focused back in on the group, feeling dread in the pit of her stomach. She might love her new family, but Pandora was right, in a way.

She had no choice in the matter. She *was* pretty much a caged rat.

2

Because donuts are fucking delicious, that's why, Pandora said angrily. *And this is supposed to be a "me" day. You got yesterday...and the day before that... and the day before that.*

Yeah, and you know why? Katie shot back. *Because it's my goddamned body!*

No, it is now our *goddamned body,* she argued. *Have you forgotten that regardless of whether* you *like it, you have to share it with me? Have you forgotten that I am a big part of the reason you still* have *a body that breathes? Hmmm?*

You are being unreasonable, Katie replied. *Sure, you have to be in there. You have no choice and neither do I, but for God's sake, you do* not *get to claim a day of the week from me. My physical body is the only thing I have to hold on to, and I am not going to let you ruin it with fat and cholesterol. It won't be good for either of us if I die of a damn stroke.*

You won't die of a stroke. Pandora scoffed. *Maybe a claw through the chest, but I take care of everything else. With my powers, there is no reason that you can't hand your stomach over to me every once in a while. I mean, ninety-nine percent of the women on this planet would kill for someone inside them who could get rid of fat and let them eat anything they wanted in the process.* Most *women would have run out and bought every piece of junk food on the market.*

Yes, well, I am not "most women," now am I? Katie replied. *I have a little bit more self-respect than to sit at some donut shop and eat them out of stock. Did you ever think that maybe, just maybe, that was fucking embarrassing? No you didn't, because you don't have to watch mothers cover their children's eyes as they lead them past me, or the snide looks from men walking past. You just sit there drowning in your godforsaken sprinkles.*

I don't really like the sprinkled ones, Pandora admitted. *I didn't want to tell you and upset the apple cart.*

Katie sighed. *You are impossible.*

Well, Pandora said, sniffing around. *How about the soaps, then? They won't make you fat.*

Just then there was a knock on Katie's door—she had left it open to let the air in instead of being closed up in there like a cave—and she turned and smiled at Eric. He was watching her curiously, obviously understanding that she was having an argument with her demon.

"Hey." Katie smiled. "What's up?"

"I thought I would come and see if you wanted to watch a couple episodes of *Days of Long Since Past?*" he asked with a half-grin.

Yes, yes, yes, Pandora squealed. *I love that show, and we are SO behind.*

You bitch, Katie said. You *did that. I don't know how, but you set that up.*

Okay, I am capable of a lot of things, but mind control is sadly not one of them, Pandora told her. *If I could control minds, don't you think all the men in this house would be dancing around us naked right now? I mean, even the priest. I bet he has a tight body under that trench coat. Hell, he probably even has a big—*

Stop, Katie said. *Please God, don't say another word. If I go watch the soaps, will you drop whatever disgusting thing you were going to say next?*

I accept your compromise, Pandora agreed. *See? That wasn't so bad.*

"Yeah, sure!" Katie said, smiling at Eric.

She put down her book and followed Eric out of the room, just glad that Pandora had stopped talking.

The demon knew exactly how to get her way because to Katie, watching a few soaps was a hell of a lot better than having a picture of a naked Damian floating around in her head. She was either going to have to start just giving in at the beginning, or get used to the vulgar porno that Pandora would constantly send through her brain. It was a no-win situation for her, but a win every time for Pandora. She figured there were probably worse things she'd agreed to than having to watch her favorite soap with her teammate.

At least her demon was helpful when she was really needed.

When they got out to the main area, Katie walked into the kitchen and made some popcorn—this time without the sugar on it. She wondered if Pandora was going to protest but she didn't, which was good because Katie was ready to cancel the whole thing. When the popcorn was done, she walked back out to the main area to find Jeremy had joined the party.

"Oh, hey." Katie smiled. "You turn into a soap opera addict like the rest of us?"

"No," Jeremy said unconvincingly. "I just really wanted to know what happened with Old Man Alvers, that's all."

"Mmmhmm," Katie said, handing him the popcorn. "Personally, I think they are going to kill him off."

"I don't," Eric said. "I think they're going to hook him up with one of the younger girls as like a sugar daddy thing. There are plenty of gold-diggers in that bunch."

"Ew." Katie shivered. "That is gross. I think the man has passed his prime on daytime television. He was on *Around the World* for like thirty years, or something insane. He needs to let it go. He is now the crazy old man on the show, and that is always a death sentence for these guys."

"Maybe it's just because he's a crazy old man in real life." Eric laughed. "I saw a picture of him at the Daytime Television awards. He was wearing a red and gold pinstriped suit, and had a twenty-year-old on his arm. But not some blonde bimbo...she was maybe twenty, and looked like she had been in his basement since she was twelve."

"Oh, God," Jeremy and Katie groaned in unison, wincing and laughing at the same time.

"That is terrible," Katie exclaimed, choking on her popcorn. "Like seriously terrible."

"Oh, shush." Eric sat up in his chair. "It's coming on."

Everyone stopped and stared at the screen, excited to watch the show. Katie actually started to relax, and figured it wasn't a half-bad way to spend her afternoon. She really wanted to be productive, but "productive" just didn't seem to be in her vocabulary lately.

She *had* been kind of aloof since LA. She wasn't alone, though—Calvin had been the same way, only a little livelier in personality…not that Katie had been all that bubbly to begin with.

Either way, she was enjoying herself right now, and she needed to learn to not feel bad about that.

No matter what was going on in the world around them.

―――――

They sat there and watched four hours' worth of soap operas. Pandora was thrilled, but when the last one was over Katie was more than ready to get something to eat.

She stood up, stretched, and yawned, looking around the room.

The guys had ordered pizza. "Well, guys, as much as I enjoy spending culinary time with you, I really can't do the pizza thing again. I'm going to get some real food."

"Pizza is in the food pyramid," Calvin commented through a full mouth from the table.

"Yeah," Eric added. "And the Teenage Mutant Ninja Turtles ate it all the time, so it can't be that bad, right?"

"Yeah, no. I won't base my nutritional intake on four mutant turtles." Katie shrugged.

"They were heroes," Jeremy yelled.

"Yeah, and so am I," Katie retorted. "For walking away from the third straight night of pizza." She waved with her fingers. "Have fun, guys. I will see you later."

"Your loss." Calvin shrugged, then pointed to one of the boxes. "Hand that shit here, since she isn't grabbing any."

Katie shook her head and went to her room to change her clothes.

She knew where she wanted to go but she didn't want to get Pandora too excited, so she stayed quiet.

When she was dressed—with make-up and everything —she headed down the elevator and out the front doors. She wanted to check on Joshua before she left for the night.

As she stepped out into the warm air, a familiar voice greeted her.

"Beautiful Katie," Mamacita said. "Where are you going, all dolled up?"

"I'm taking myself to dinner." She smiled. "You look fantastic as well in that executive-level suit. I barely even recognized you."

Mamacita smirked. "You have to *look* professional before you can *be* professional."

"I was just going in to check on Joshua," Katie replied.

"Oh, he's fine." She looked at the shop and then returned her gaze to Katie. "He is getting used to the new room they built him to sleep in. He likes it, although I can't seem to keep him off the forge."

"I won't complain."

"He was just getting ready to call it a day when I came out to get something from the car." Mamacita pointed to her vehicle.

"Oh. Well, I'll just leave him alone then. I know how nervous he gets when I come in."

"He does, but only because he wants to make you happy," Mamacita replied.

"Right." Katie chewed on her lip a moment. "Oh, and I'd like to thank you for straightening out the orders and everything else here with the business."

"Not a problem." She nodded. "It's something I've become good at over time. I wasn't always well-to-do. I started from nothing."

"I appreciate you using your skills for us. Well, you have a great night." Katie sighed. "I'm gonna hit the road."

"Be careful out there." She waved to Katie.

Katie waved back, noticing Korbin heading toward Joshua's building. She thought it was strange that he was going back over, but figured he had something pressing he had to get off his mind before he could call it a day...or whatever Korbin did when everyone else finished their day. She shrugged, figuring there was no reason to even think about it. Korbin did what he did, and always for a reason.

He has no idea who he is messing with. Pandora snickered. *I give him a month, only because he's hard-headed.*

Wait, what? Katie replied, looking around. *Okay, what the hell is going on?*

Seriously, this place is like its own soap opera, Pandora replied.

A paranormal soap opera? Katie corrected.

Yeah, that, Pandora agreed.

So, you aren't going to tell me?

You'll figure it out eventually. Pandora giggled. *Now let's go to dinner. I'm freaking starving, and I think going to Bootlegger is a perfect idea.*

How did you...

I'm in your head, remember? Pandora pointed out. *And now that I know, you can't take it back. I already have a hankering for ravioli and steak.*

I decided on it for you anyway. Katie sighed. *Figured you were right; you deserve a day here and there to eat what you want.*

Aw, she really does care, Pandora cooed.

BUT! I am not getting as much as last time, and you cannot have one day every week, Katie warned. *And you better turn it into muscle—and muscle I can actually use.*

Why would I ever betray your trust when you are feeding me delicious food?

Were you like this when you were here outside of a body? Katie asked, climbing into the SUV. *I mean, were you obsessed with food?*

It has been a long time since I walked on this plane, Pandora explained. *Last time I was here, there was no food like this. I mean, there were restaurants, but they were dusty, and no one ever cooked food like that.*

That's right, that's why you used that Italian woman, Katie said, rolling her eyes. *I guess it would be exciting if you had never experienced it before, but still... You have got to go easy on me tonight.*

Katie drove out of the garage in the huge SUV and turned down the sand-covered drive to the main highway.

She sighed as she drove along, thinking about her tiny Altima from college. She missed having a car, and definitely missed the freedom of going anywhere she wanted to, even though she rarely did that.

Knowing that she had wasted all that time in college

when she could have been seeing the world made her mad, but at the same time, had she done that she wouldn't have ended up where she was. She wasn't sure what was worse: being a broke wandering hippy, or being a badass demon slayer.

Both had their negatives, but she could see a few positives to her place in Korbin's Killers for the first time since she had arrived.

At least she hadn't ended up with a lazy-ass demon like some of the others—though she was jealous of the fact that there was quiet in their lives.

You have quiet too! Pandora exclaimed.

God, get out of my head. Katie groaned. *Can I not be alone in here for five minutes?*

Hey, it's not like I enjoy being in here with all your melodrama and "woe is me" bullshit, she said. *But you're fucking loud, and I can't tune it out.*

Well, sorry, but there is nothing I can do about that, Katie said. *Just be glad you aren't in the priest's head.*

Oh, lord...the prayers, Pandora griped. *I would definitely beg for exorcism. Even torture would be better than hearing prayers all day every day.*

See, things could be worse! Katie replied. *Shut up about my thoughts, for God's sake. I'm just glad I don't have to hear yours.*

You would exorcise yourself, Pandora quipped.

Katie pulled up to Bootlegger and parked the car.

Then she sat there for a moment thinking about what she was about to get herself into. Surely, they thought she was a freak for eating all that food, but that didn't bother her as much as her lack of self-control when Pandora got rid of the full feeling.

All right, we're here. Katie sighed. *Remember what I said… we are* not *gorging ourselves like last time.*

Mmmhmm, Pandora agreed, her insubstantial fingers crossed behind her back.

I mean it! Katie put her foot down…metaphorically.

The only problem was, Pandora didn't give a shit.

3

D amian whistled as he walked down the hall with his hands in his pockets.

He had some sermons to take care of and some praying to do, then some business to take care of. He wasn't in any rush, though. It was the weekend; the house was quiet, the sun was shining, and he had been listening to Tony Bennett in his room all morning while getting ready.

It was one of those days where he couldn't seriously put a lot of effort into anything, but that was okay. He was ready to relax a bit.

As he passed Katie's room, he smiled and stopped for a moment when he again heard moaning coming from the other side of the door.

He reached up to knock but stopped short, thinking about the last time he had heard her in there.

This was the same exact miserable moan as before.

He put his hand back in his pocket and turned to walk

away, then stopped again. He laughed to himself, picturing her in there with a huge stomach, rolling around on the bed in misery. She didn't seem to learn her lessons very well, and it made him wonder what she had been like as a kid.

He bet she had stuck her hand on the stove at least twice when she was little. He shook his head and turned back to the door, reaching up and knocking lightly on it. He stood back and waited for her to answer, but all he heard was a loud groan.

He laughed again, but covered his mouth with his fist to stifle the sound.

"Did you go out to eat last night?" he yelled through the door.

He already knew the answer, and he could guess where she had gone since she had announced she was leaving before she went. He couldn't help but tease her, though.

Anyone who would do that to herself twice deserved for him to pick at her at least a little bit. He felt like Katie was a little sister, and what did big brothers do best?

They picked on their little sisters, and tormented them until they were completely embarrassed. He was definitely up to that.

"Bootlegger..." she groaned in response. "*You fuckers...*"

Damian laughed loudly when he heard more moans.

He had been spot-on. He stood there for a moment, contemplating what to say next. After a few minutes, he cleared his throat and spoke loudly.

'I'll come back later. I don't need to see what a beached whale looks like a second time."

He jumped slightly when something heavy hit the door

and snickered, knowing she had picked up whatever was closest and thrown it.

He walked away, knowing that he had tormented her enough, and went into the living room. Eric was the only one there. "Hey, Eric."

Eric smiled. "Hey. Is Katie up?"

"Uh, yeah, but I think you probably would do better leaving her alone for now." Damian chuckled.

"Why?" Eric asked, confused.

"She ate an entire cow last night. She won't be rolling out for a while."

"All right," Eric said slowly. "It doesn't seem like she is going to learn her lesson."

"No, no I don't think she will."

"What are you doing today?" Eric asked.

"Just enjoying the day." Damian wiped a hand over his chin. "I think I'll go for a walk."

"Okay," Eric said, furrowing his brow. "I still can't get past how weird everyone is here."

"Get used to it. It only gets stranger." Damian turned toward the stairs and waved over his shoulder.

———

Eric watched Damian disappear down the stairs, sighing as the door shut behind him. He was the only one left, and he wasn't sure what to do with his free time.

He was still used to the outside world, but his free time there had been only half-free. He shrugged his shoulders and got up from the chair, walking toward Katie's room.

How bad could it be, right? He figured Damian had

overplayed her distress. He went to her door and knocked, then stood back and waited for her friendly hello.

All he heard was a loud bang on the door, and her groaning like a monster inside. Eric jumped back and looked around before taking off down the hall back to the living room.

Apparently Damian had *understated* what was going on. There was no way he was going to bother whatever creature was behind that door.

Katie laid on the bed, rubbing her hand in circles over her stomach. She had a very large food baby in there; she was pretty sure this one was bigger than the first time.

She wasn't sure how it could possibly be worse, but she was willing to bet serious money it was, dammit, and she regretted every glorious moment of it.

Even Pandora had been oddly quiet that morning, not feeling too hot herself even though none of that food had gone into *her* stomach.

It serves you right, Katie groaned. *I told you no, but you kept pushing. You made me feel terribly guilty.*

Don't blame me, witch. Pandora retorted. *You are a person too. You have the ability to tell me no and actually follow through with it. The truth was, you didn't want to stop. You liked fulfilling your cravings—eating sugar and carbs and fat without having to worry about it. I can only spike your metabolism so high. At this point you are just going to have to wait it out.*

Can you at least help me nap through it? Katie sniveled.

Sure, why not? Pandora replied. *I could make you suffer—*

which is my specialty—but I am tired of hearing you complain. It is causing me to suffer, not something I am particularly fond of. You yes, me no.

Gee, thanks, I... Katie passed out.

You said you wanted to sleep. Pandora chuckled, yawning herself.

Katie was out, probably sleeping more deeply than she had most nights recently. Hell, this was probably even better than the time they had given her a sedative before taking out her tonsils when she was eight.

She didn't move a muscle, not even to turn on her side. Her head was tilted back and her mouth was open, and the sound of her snoring filled the room.

After a few minutes of trying to rest, Pandora had enough and forced her body over onto her side. She laid like that for several hours, not dreaming or restless, just letting her body work through the disgusting place she was in.

When she did finally wake up, she looked over sleepily at the clock. It was early afternoon.

Katie sat up in the bed and yawned, stretching her arms high over her head. She felt much better than she had before. She rolled over to get a little circulation in her limbs, then stood up. She grabbed a change of clothes, brushed her teeth, and walked back out of the bathroom in a wonderfully rested state.

Her demon was better than sleeping pills.

Wake up, she said to Pandora.

Why? Pandora groaned.

Because you and I have somewhere to go, Katie told her.

Donuts? Pandora asked with enthusiasm.

Uh, no, Katie said. *We are good on food at this point, thanks.*

Then what the hell can be important enough to wake me up? she asked.

We are going car shopping! Katie said excitedly.

Really? Pandora asked, her voice now fully awake. *Yes!*

I know exactly where I want to go first.

Porsche? Pandora asked interestedly.

Precisely, Katie replied.

Now there *is sex on four wheels.*

Katie snuck out of the house before anyone caught her and grabbed the third SUV down in the row.

Almost everyone was gone from the house that day, which made her secret mission that much easier.

She wasn't sure if what she was doing was allowed, but she figured that after going through all the trouble of getting a fake identity, she would rather apologize than ask permission.

She headed to Redwood Drive, where the Porsche dealership was located. Katie didn't know a bunch about cars, but there was a black car on display that she had seen a million times and wanted to know more about.

When she pulled up a salesman greeted her in his very expensive suit, perfect hair, and gentle voice.

"How can we help you today?" he asked.

"I was wondering, what is that car you have on display?" Katie asked, aware that perhaps she hadn't dressed appropriately for going expensive car shopping.

"Well, that is one of my favorites. That is the 2015 918 Spyder Hybrid," he replied. "They stopped making them after that year, but *I* think it should be a staple."

"Very beautiful," she said. "How much is it?"

26

"That particular model comes with all the bells and whistles 2015 offered." He smiled. "We are selling it at nine hundred thousand, which is fifty above the base model cost."

She had *definitely* not dressed up enough.

"Wow!" Katie exclaimed, trying not to show her shock. "May I take a look at it?"

"Of course," he said. "Let us know if you need any help."

Katie smiled. "Thank you."

She walked over to the car and let out a deep sigh; it was exactly what she had imagined driving around the city. It was sleek and glittery black, and looked almost like something Batman would drive around Gotham. Vegas was her Gotham, but a car like that was a bit more than what she was looking for pricewise.

This is amazing, Pandora gushed. *My lips are wet already.*

I don't want to know what you mean by that, Katie told her. *But I do know that it's too expensive for me. We have a business to run.*

Your business will be fine. Pandora scoffed. *We should be treating ourselves, lest we die tomorrow.*

Is that what all your ridiculous choices come from? The fear you will be back in hell any day? Katie asked.

Pandora sniffed. *No, that's just the donuts.*

No, Katie said firmly. *This is too much. Let's move on.*

Finnnnne. Pandora griped. *I would have orgasmed every time we drove that car.*

Katie jumped back in the SUV and headed to West Sahara Avenue to check out the Aston Martin dealership.

She had seen a Vanquish one time at a car show in Las Vegas and had loved the look of the car ever since.

She hadn't checked on it in a long time, though, so she had no real idea how much it cost or if they even made it anymore—but she was dead-set on finding out.

When they pulled up, she spotted a full row of them in almost every color offered. She had gotten out of the car and started to walk over to them when a salesman approached her.

"Good afternoon." He smiled. "How can I help you today?"

"I just came to see how deep your Vanquish selection was." Katie returned his smile.

He waved to the row of cars. "Well, as you can see, we have a nice selection right now. Or, we can order one to your specifications if we don't have what you want in stock." He glanced at her clothes. "You can also check out our used car area, where there are some older versions."

"Gotcha." Katie nodded. "If you don't mind, I'd like to just walk around.

"Absolutely. Let us know if you need anything." He smiled again before going back into the dealership office.

Katie wandered over to the black one at the end of the row and peeked inside. It had a leather interior, manual transmission, beautiful mahogany accents, and a dashboard she imagined lit up like you were in a spaceship. She walked around the other side and looked at the price point on the window.

She swallowed hard when she read the three-hundred-thousand-dollar price tag.

How about this beauty? Pandora asked. *Huh? You know you want to take it home right now.*

It's still too much, she declared. *I could buy a house or two for that amount. I just can't stomach that price for a car.*

You are seriously *cramping my car style here*, Pandora chided. *I mean, what the hell? I know you have twice that much in your drawer at home.*

That isn't the point, Katie told her.

What is *the point, then?* Pandora asked as Katie made her way back to the SUV.

The point is, no matter how rich I am, I can't handle paying that much for a car, Katie replied. *I'd rather send my mom the majority of it and drive a dang Toyota.*

Don't even say that, Pandora gasped. *You are going to hurt my fragile sensibilities.*

You will survive, Katie grumped. *I'm not done yet, don't worry. I am going to find the car I want and feel comfortable paying for.*

You mean you are going to be boring and buy a minivan, Pandora grunted.

What the hell would I do with a minivan? Katie laughed. *I would much rather get like a Jeep SUV of some sort.*

Oh, God, Pandora moaned. *I am stuck in car buyer hell with uptight panty girl who wants to buy a car a soccer mom would haul around her five kids in.*

No kids for me, obviously. She sighed. *And I'm not going to buy one, I'm just saying I'd rather have that than a minivan.*

Shit, I'd rather have a clown car than a minivan, Pandora exclaimed. *This is the first century that I will be able to have a car, and I can't even get you to shell out enough to make it a good one.*

You are being impossible, Katie scolded, pulling out of the parking lot. *I have a plan, so you need to just sit back and relax. You are driving me crazy already.*

At least I'm driving in style, she grumped. *Get it? DRIVING in style. No? Never mind.*

That was a terrible joke, Katie replied. *Like...terrible.*

Yeah, well, you have taken my spunk away, she said, pouting like a child.

I am just going to go home if you don't lay off, Katie warned. *We can continue driving the super-secret-looking blacked-out SUV.*

No. Pandora sighed. *I'll behave, but you better have a good plan. Leaving those two cars behind was just crazy. Why did you go top-of-the-line first? Seriously, are you just doing a reverse temptation on me? Because, if you are, it sucks. Not that it wouldn't impress the hell out of me that you are learning how to be a bitch, but I'll certainly torture your titties to extinction if I find out that's true.*

I have a good plan, she argued, ignoring the rest of Pandora's rant. *Just wait and see.*

Katie sure hoped Dealer Number Three was a hit.

4

K atie pulled into the Ferrari dealership and smiled—half in relief—as Pandora whistled.

She got out of the car, and instead of looking around the lot, she went straight into the building to talk to a salesman since she wasn't very familiar with Ferrari. There was a younger guy, tall, thin build, standing at the front waiting for her to come in.

He smiled. "Welcome to Ferrari. How can we help you today?"

"I am in the market for a car, and I thought this would be a good place to come," Katie explained.

"And that it is," he agreed. "Come on." He gestured. "I'll tell you a little about Ferrari, and we can walk around the show room."

"Perfect," she said, following him down the hall into a large open space with a number of exotic cars.

"Ferrari was officially recognized in 1947 when the

first one was completed and ready for the road," he told her, walking along the line of older Ferraris on display.

"Enzo Ferrari was a race car maker and driver, but in 1939 he quit and started his own business, Auto Avio Costruzioni. The cars were still for racing, but geared more toward your weekend gentleman racers. When the war hit, though, all production came to a halt. When the war was over, Mr. Ferrari built the 125-S which went on that very month to win the Rome Grand Prix. Ferrari boasts over five hundred wins with its vehicles."

"Wow." Katie looked at the pictures, reaching up to one that had what she guessed was Rome in the background. "I didn't realize they were that far into racing."

"Very much so." He smiled. "Once that started happening demand for Ferrari cars became overwhelming for Enzo, so he sold fifty percent of the company to Fiat. They helped move the production along fast and efficiently. In 1988 Mr. Ferrari died, and Fiat's ownership in the company grew to ninety percent. But we still make the genuine Ferrari car Enzo made first—and that brings me to the California model, the car I pictured you driving as soon as you drove up."

The salesman stopped in front of the last car on the showroom floor and Katie's eyes got big. It was smooth, sleek, and absolutely gorgeous. It was the exact car that she could see herself driving around Las Vegas in.

The question was, was it affordable?

"This is the Ferrari California T," he said. "On the inside it's for the gentleman—or gentle*lady*—weekend racer. But the outside is luxurious, and it will give you a smooth ride anywhere your heart desires."

Wow! Pandora exclaimed. *He is good.*

Tell me about it, Katie replied.

He tells a story about a car like he is talking about a woman, Pandora continued. *It's kind of hot.*

"This is a beautiful car," Katie admitted, her eyes sweeping the lines of the car.

"That it definitely is," he agreed. "My first luxury vehicle was a California T. I still have it parked in my garage, though I don't drive it as often as I would like."

She turned to look at him. "What do you drive the rest of the time?" she asked.

"A Fiat." He shrugged. "It's ecologically more responsible and my wife is a climate change researcher, so she gets on me for the cars."

"That will do it." Katie nodded in understanding. "So what colors does it come in?"

"There are endless colors." He waved a hand to show a few on the floor. "And we can get into that all when you decide that you want to purchase it—and trust me, you *will* want to purchase it by the time the day is over."

Yeah, he just told you what the hell you will do. Pandora snickered. *If he wasn't showing you a car, I would say kick him in his machismo for being too forward.*

I bet that line works more often than not. Katie laughed. *Get it in your head that the car is already yours. It's much harder to back out of something you have an emotional attachment to, and he is definitely creating that for me.*

"What are you driving now?" he asked.

"Oh, my company vehicle." She wrinkled her nose. "I haven't picked a car to buy, so the boss lets me drive the SUV."

"That's cool of him." He smiled. "I have to say though, I would feel so limited if I didn't have my car. It's literally a tool for getting out of bad situations."

Katie walked around the car, continuing to speak as she looked at it from all directions. "I feel pretty naked without a car, which is why I am here. To get one, I mean, but it won't be stuck away in a garage somewhere. It will be used on a regular basis to get me either into bad situations or out of them."

"Touché." He laughed. "I seem to do both myself, as well."

"That's what makes life fun," she murmured.

"Come with me," he replied, and waved a hand as he started walking down the hallway.

Katie followed him to the outdoor show area, where he brought her to a red California T, top down and ready to go. She smiled and walked around it once more, coming to a stop next to him.

"Now, my suggestion would be to custom-order yours so you get everything that you want," he said, handing her the keys. "But I figured you might want to *drive* one first."

She accepted the keys, her eyes wide. "I'm nervous," She laughed.

He opened the driver's door for her. "Don't be. You'll see how well you fit into it."

He closed the door once he made sure she was in, and walked around to the passenger side to climb in himself.

He took two Ferrari ball caps out of the glove compartment and handed one to Katie. She chuckled and put it on as he did the same.

"This should keep our hair out of our eyes." He grinned;

both of them knew that was so much bullshit. It was the art of the deal, and he was helping her sign onto Team Ferrari.

Katie started the car and rolled her eyes in ecstasy; now she knew what Pandora meant about her lips being wet. The car purred to her, and begged her to drive it.

She slowly pulled out of the dealership and onto the road, gripping the steering wheel tightly. The salesman, who was wearing a perfectly pressed suit, looked at her and chuckled.

"Why don't you take a deep breath and open her up?" he suggested. "You can stop white-knuckling the steering wheel. We have insurance for a reason."

Everything felt so comfortable and nice that she didn't know how she could walk away from the thing. Her body molded into the seats, and although it had originally been created with a man in mind, the whole thing fit her like a glove. She relaxed a bit and glanced at the salesman.

"All right," Katie said, "talk to me. Tell me about this car."

"Well, it comes in at just under two hundred and fifteen thousand, depending on what you include with it," he began. "It has five hundred and two horses under the hood."

Damn, Pandora said. *That's even more horses than I'd care to have between my legs.*

Holy shit, Pandora! That is so fucking gross.

I'm kidding, for fuck's sake, Pandora replied. *Don't slide on your prude panties! Lighten the hell up.*

When you talk about screwing horses, it's hard to lighten up, Katie argued, taking a right and enjoying the feel of the acceleration.

Well? Pandora asked.

Well what? Katie replied.

What do you think about this car? she asked. *I have to admit, it is* way *cooler than I thought it would be. It also fits your style perfectly. How does it drive?*

Like you are navigating through the clouds, Katie replied. *I am pretty much in love with this car.*

Yessss, Pandora hissed. *I knew you would be, the moment you got into the thing. It's no Spyder, but it's definitely hot enough for me.*

Katie drove down the Strip and back to the dealership, pulling the car up in front. The salesman showed her a couple of cool things on the inside, then took the keys and helped her from the car. She stood back and looked it over, knowing that it was definitely the car for her.

"So," he asked. "What do you think?"

"I think I am in love with the thing," She laughed, and the sales guy glanced at her.

"Everyone has that response after driving it." He chuckled. "When people think Ferrari they think race cars, so they are expecting a loud hard-to-control car, but these California T's are made for the customer who just wants a car to drive. They are built to be a daily part of your routine. The convertible gives it that California feel, which I love since I am from there."

"Nice," Katie replied. "I love Cali. I was actually just in San Diego and LA for business."

"Were you there when the cemetery was vandalized?" he asked, just making conversation.

"I was, but not real close," she said, feeling a twinge of fear in her belly.

Liar, liar, pants on fire… Wait, that's what I'm supposed to be working on. Keep up the good work!

"Well, that's a good thing. From what people are telling me, whatever did it was something they had never seen before, and a lot of people died."

"That's what I heard too," Katie said, wanting to change the subject.

"Anyway, we are safe here in Vegas. Do you have any questions that I can answer?" the salesman asked, clapping his hands together—or rather damn near rubbing them together in glee, already counting his commission in his head.

"I can't really think of any," she responded.

"If you were to buy the car, would you be financing with us?" he continued down his path of closing, closing, closing.

"No," she answered. "I will be paying in cash."

"Well, that makes everything a lot less complicated." He pointed out the closer entrance to the building. "It will be just as easy as you sitting down with me and designing the car, signing a couple of papers, and coming back to pick it up when it is ready."

Katie smiled. "I guess we should get started, then."

"Excellent!" he exclaimed. "Let's go to my office, and you can start looking over the options."

Katie nodded and followed him inside and around the corner to his office in the back. The walls were glass, but the room was large. Katie wondered if every salesman had an office like his.

When they walked in he pulled out a chair in front of his desk, motioning for her to have a seat.

"I'm sorry," he said. "What is your name?"

"Ka—*Elizabeth*," she said. *Damn fake identities!*

"Nice to meet you, Elizabeth." He pushed her chair in. "My name is Brian."

"Nice to meet, you, Brian," She laid her purse on the desk.

"Okay," he said, sitting down behind his desk and turning one of two screens toward her. "We'll go over all the different options you have for the car. I can explain anything you don't understand, and we can get the order sent off to the manufacturer so they can customize your car."

"All right," she said, sitting up straight and looking at the screen.

"First things first: what color do you want the exterior to be?" he asked.

Katie had thought she would choose black, but when she looked through the swatches and California Blue came up, she changed her mind. It was almost the perfect mixture of grey and aquamarine.

"California Blue," she said definitely. "Hands down. No contest whatsoever."

"An excellent choice," he agreed, typing it in. "Let's move down to your wheels and calipers. You have several choices for the rims, some in silver and a couple in black. You can press the different options on your screen to see how they look."

Katie went through each rim, and the matte-black Grigio wheels caught her eye. They were a good contrast to the shiny blue. After that she picked out a caliper that was the same color as the car, and opted for a replacement wheel kit for the trunk. That ensured that if anything were to happen, she had a spare tire in the back specially made for the California T.

"That is looking really nice," Brian said. "Okay, next we have the body components. The shield option is completely cosmetic. It puts the Ferrari shield of honor right next to your mirrors."

Katie nodded. "I like how that looks."

Yummmm...

"Good, and from there we have the sport exhaust system, which I highly recommend since the car is so powerful," he continued, watching her click on it. "We will skip the black pillars and move on to the front grill. Now, you can have the whole thing chrome, the whole thing black, or you can do chrome-tipped so it's not overly shiny but has an air of luxury to it."

"I like the chrome-tipped," Katie decided, selecting that option.

"The special handling package changes the look," he warned.

"Yeah, I don't like that. I'm going to keep it how it was," she replied. "I'm going to go with dual suspension and the Anti-stone chipping, but what is 'AFS?'"

"AFS is a system we're pretty proud of." He looked at her. "What it does is change your nighttime driving head-lights to whatever brightness and angle you need, depending on your location, speed, and handling. It also engages the lights anytime you park, to avoid running up on curbs in the dark."

"That's cool," she said, clicking it. "And the high emotion-low emission is..."

"This is also a nice feature," he said, watching her choose on the heated windows and the front and rear parking cameras. "It creates a system where the car will run optimally, and therefore it uses less power than if it were running without the system."

"All right," she said, clicking on the option, along with electric mirrors inside and out.

"Now comes the fun part—the interior." He laughed.

"Oh, that's easy." She smiled. "I would like all black, with the black gear shift, diamond back design, and black leather on the doors."

"Those are excellent and very sleek choices," he agreed. "Just a couple more things. Do you want a CD player, or are you okay with USB plugin for music?"

"I don't need a CD slot as long as I have plenty of places to plug things in," Katie replied.

"There will definitely be plenty of places," he told her. "Now, last question…do you want this delivered here or to your house?"

"Oh, here, please."

He smiled. "Okay, then we are all set. Once you pay, I can send in the order."

"Sure." She pulled out an envelope of cash, looked at the final number, and pointed to the screen. "Everything is in this final price, including tax and title fees?"

"Yes," he told her.

Katie started counting. He tried to keep his face still, making his best effort to not look surprised by the money stacking up on his desk. He printed out some paperwork, made a deposit slip for the safe, and handed her a pen.

She took the pen from him and smiled.

"Okay, once you sign these we are good to go," he said. "I will have to check if there is a model that is similarly equipped in the US, that we can customize to your specs. If so, your car will be here in a week or ten days. If not, it will be eight or more weeks coming from Italy. I'll let you know as soon as I do some research."

NOW we'll have us some fun, Pandora cooed.

5

"Do you like this?" Korbin asked, holding up a swatch of cloth.

"Are we picking out curtains together?" Calvin teased.

"No, you idiot." he chuckled. "It's for the shop. As much as possible, we want to try to make it look like a house."

"Oh, well, then yeah, I like that," he said. "It's masculine with the dark blue and gold. No man wants to walk into a brothel and be surrounded by pink and fluffy."

"A brothel?" Korbin asked nonchalantly. "What makes you say that?"

Calvin looked up at him and raised one eyebrow. Korbin sighed and nodded, tired of thinking about stupid details like fabric for the fucking windows.

He put the swatch down and leaned back in his chair, rubbing his face.

He was about done with everything to do with the cover up. He just wanted the business—that was it, no sparkles or vanity. Just *simple*, unlike most things in his damn life. Before he could go back to work, though, the phone rang.

"Hello?" he answered.

"Hey, it's Charlotte," the reporter said.

"Hi there," Korbin replied. "Hold on, let me put you on speaker. Calvin's here too."

Korbin looked at Calvin and mouthed Charlotte's name, watching him knowingly nod his head. He clicked on the speaker and pulled out a pad of paper and a pen. He was a note taker, especially with so much on his mind.

"Hey there, Charlotte," Calvin greeted her.

"Hey, Calvin," she replied. "So, I have an update for you guys. I've been checking up on the politician, but he hasn't done anything strange...yet. Currently I am working his background, but it's going to come up with his human record, not anything demon-related."

"You need to be careful," Korbin warned her. "He is willing to kill anyone who stands in his way."

"I know. I'm inquisitive," she replied, "not suicidal."

"I need to get out of this place," Eric told them. He was sitting across from Jeremy and Katie in the living room. "I need to feel normal again. You know, walk the streets like a normal person."

"Whatcha got in mind?" Jeremy asked.

"I was thinking we go to downtown Las Vegas and play around for a while," Eric replied. "You know, do as the tourists do."

"I'm up for it," Katie agreed.

"Me too," Jeremy replied.

"Awesome!" Eric exclaimed. "Okay, we gotta make ourselves look different. There are bound to be a lot of people down there, and none of us want to get caught by someone we know."

"Sounds smart." Katie stood up. "Give me twenty, and we'll meet back out here?"

"Yeah," Eric said.

"I mean, don't go too crazy trying to change things up," Jeremy offered. "Most of downtown is tourists, and most locals avoid it like the plague. Just make sure you look different than you did in your prior life."

"That won't be a problem." Katie laughed. "Much of me has changed since everything happened. I'm pretty sure my own mother wouldn't recognize me at this point."

"Better to be safe than sorry, though," Eric replied. "It would be just our luck if we didn't do something. We would definitely run into someone we knew, and then there would be mind-erasing and a scene. That is just not what I'm looking for tonight."

"I mean, there are so many tourists," Jeremy said. "There are bound to be some of them who look like us. We should be able to blend right in, with the right hair and civilian clothes."

"You would think so." Katie sighed, thinking back to her review of the social websites over the last year when she couldn't be strong. "But like Eric said, it's better to be safe than sorry. My 'death' has already put my family and friends through enough. The last thing I want is to have to erase their memories because of me."

"You are absolutely right," Jeremy agreed. "We all lost people when we switched to Korbin's Killers, and I wouldn't want to put my family and friends through anything else either."

"All right." Katie waved to the guys. "I'm going to go get ready. I'll meet you guys back out here shortly, and we can inspect each other's disguises."

"You should wear a beard." Jeremy laughed. "You can be the Bearded Lady."

"Uh, I don't think so." Katie laughed and walked toward her room.

Katie made it to her room and closed the door, then rummaged through her closet. She wasn't sure what the guys had in mind for the evening. She didn't want to be too fancy, but at the same time she didn't want to be left out of going into places on the Strip because she wore jeans shorts and a tank top.

She pulled out a pair of wide-leg black dress pants and a sexy black top and changed her clothes. When she was done, she walked into the bathroom and arranged her hair differently than she had done it before. She pulled it back in a ponytail, but created "the bump" in front.

She put on some makeup, and stood back to stare at her reflection in the mirror. She looked at herself from all angles, surprised at how toned her entire body was. She had known she would be in shape from all the training, but dang! She had "guns."

You look hot, Pandora told her. *I'm proud of you for picking this outfit.*

"Thanks." Katie sighed. "You know, I think I could go out on the Strip with no makeup, in jeans, and anyone who might or did know me would pass right by without another thought. No one is going to think I'm that girl anymore. I'm taller, more muscular, and have tits the size of Texas. They will notice my boobs before they ever look at my face.

Bahaha, Pandora howled. *"Tits the size of Texas!"*

Yeah, Katie bitched, adjusting her shirt. *My tops and bras don't fit right anymore. I told you to leave the boobs alone.*

Honey, Pandora explained, *Texas is as big as France. You're no bigger than Arkansas, at the most.*

I was exaggerating, Katie snapped. *They seem huge to me, because I have always been just average in the breast department. Now I can't even see my fucking toes, and not only are they enormous, but they are perky—like I need steel plates to hide my nipples, even with a bra and a tank top underneath what I am wearing.*

I know what we could do for a disguise, Pandora offered.

This should be interesting, Katie replied, adjusting her boobs in the mirror.

We could cut your hair, she suggested. *Give you some kind of cute and trendy haircut. That would be the icing on the cake. No one would recognize you.*

That's an interesting suggestion, Katie agreed. *I have one for you, too. Why don't you try to be celibate for a thousand years? I'm sure your body would thank me.*

Wow, Pandora said with a sniff. *A simple "no" would have been sufficient. You didn't have to be so ugly with me about it. I mean, there is a huge difference between a thousand years without any dick and cutting some of that hair off. Besides, you are a different person now, and not just on the outside. Maybe it would be good for you to lose some of it.*

No, Katie told her firmly. *I am not cutting my hair. We'll just have to make do with what I've got.*

Fine, fine, Pandora grumped. *Don't take my advice! God knows I failed the other times...except I didn't!*

Katie frowned into the mirror. *As much as I love your help on everything else, this one is non-negotiable, I'm afraid. My hair is pretty much the only thing I have left from my former life, and I'm not ready to give it up.*

Okay. Pandora sighed. *It was just a suggestion.*

"This is really good," Joshua said, taking a bite of his casserole.

"Thank you," one of the girls said. "I made it myself."

"It's nn-nnn-nice to have a home-cooked meal," he told them.

"So, Joshua," Eliza, the older girl began. "Why are these knives you make so important?"

"Yeah, how did you start making these things, anyway?" Tabby, another of the girls, asked.

"I'll be honest with you," Joshua replied. "I can't tell you everything. There are some secrets about this place and what I am doing that can't be revealed. I wish I could tell you ladies everything, though, especially since you have gone out of your way to come out here and help me."

"Gosh, it sounds like these weapons are super-secret?" Tabby exclaimed. "Why is that? I mean, can't you buy swords and knives everywhere nowadays?"

Joshua dug his fork through the casserole. He didn't

know what to say, or how much he was allowed to tell them.

They worked there, but they didn't get paid for it.

He assumed that if Katie had wanted them to know the whole truth, she would have told them herself. Still, he couldn't just push them off when they were coming here every day to help out with the business. If he were them he would have a lot more questions, including what went on next door at all hours, why they snuck out all of the time, and why the building was under high security. He figured the girls didn't really think about those things or notice them.

"Well, they are made differently than the ones you can just buy at the store," he explained.

"How?" Eliza asked.

"Well, it's a bit complicated," Joshua replied. "My family has been making them, or has known how to make them, for centuries, apparently. When my father died, I was given the tools and books and told it was of dire importance that I continue the family business. Most everything has been passed down from generation to generation in books and diaries. Normally a father would explain everything to the next generation, but he died so suddenly that it was impossible."

"Do you miss him?" Tabby asked.

"I do," Joshua admitted, looking down. "I miss him all the time, really. But I am doing what he wanted for me, and that makes me feel close to him."

"Did your dad do this too?" one of the other girls asked. "I mean, did you learn all this from him."

"Well, no, not exactly," Joshua said. "My dad, he taught

me some stuff, but he wasn't really very interested in it. He had his own way of helping out, though, and it was like what Katie and Korbin and the rest of them do."

"Which is super-secret." Tabby laughed.

"Yeah, it is." Joshua blushed. "But my grandfather…he tried to do it, but he didn't really understand everything. To be honest, neither did I when he first gave everything to me. He wasn't able to explain too much more than the basics. My father understood it, but by the time I was old enough to start doing it my father was gone. I couldn't do what my father did, because I have Asperger's Syndrome and it would be too risky. At least, that is what he used to tell me, and now I agree with him. So when it came time for me to take care of myself, I took up the other family business."

Tabby was playing with her hair. "But if your dad was dead, how did you figure out all the missing pieces?"

"I started to travel to find out what I needed to know," he said. "It was the only thing I knew to do. My father had left me money and my mother passed away soon after him, so I had to do something. I am the last person in my family, and when I die this knowledge does too. I couldn't let it die with my father."

"So where did you travel?" Tabby asked. "To like California and stuff?"

"N-n-no." He shook his head. "I went to Israel, Europe, and the United Kingdom. There were also a few places in Central and southern America and Asia that I was led to through different contacts. Oh, and there were a few stops in Egypt as well. I really just followed the trail, picking up little bits of information here and there and piecing it all together until I had the full picture. Sometimes I didn't get anything, sometimes I got a bunch of info, and sometimes I just got a clue as to where to go to next. This isn't your run-of-the-mill weapon-making, so people were very secretive."

"So what did you find out?" Tabby asked. "I mean, what is the metal used for?"

"I can't really go too deep into that," he replied. "It's not something that I am allowed to reveal. I will just say that the knowledge that I found helps to create a very special metal that harmonizes energies."

"What exactly does it do?" Eliza asked.

"Well, in a scientific explanation," he began, trying to craft something he knew they wouldn't fully understand and would never speak of in fear that they would look stupid, "ultimately what it does is unknown, but the indications I found lead me to hypothesize that the metal is very disharmonious to those whose energy is dark."

6

Katie put her phone to her ear when she saw the dealership number show up. "Hi, Elizabeth! I just wanted to let you know that your car should be arriving in just a couple of days," Brian told her. "I found one in San Diego, and they are just finishing up the additions to bring it to your spec. I'll call you when it comes in, and we'll make sure it's gassed up and ready when you get here."

"That's really great news!"

Katie pressed End and squealed, excited that she was going to have her car in a few days. She knew she wouldn't be driving it far, but just having something like her new baby was thrilling. She not only had never been able to afford something so nice, but it also made her feel a little bit more *normal*.

During the test drive she had been on cloud nine, feeling like a regular person—just driving a car with the top down through the streets of Las Vegas.

Maybe it was a stupid waste of money since she had access to the SUVs, but she didn't care. She didn't do those kinds of things *ever*, and she'd definitely never had anything that nice before.

The ride is gonna be here soon? Pandora asked.

Sure the hell is, Katie replied.

Yessss, Pandora hissed. *I can't wait to roll through Las Vegas feeling the wind in your hair, seeing all the jealousy on everyone's faces, and seeing just how much of a man-magnet this thing is going to be. I mean, you should be able to seriously pick up some dick with this thing.*

That was not a priority, Katie told her, *nor was it a consideration in buying the car.*

"Attention," Korbin announced over the loudspeaker. "We are going to be starting our team workout in exactly ten minutes. Please make sure you are dressed for PT, not combat. Thank you."

Uh oh, training time, Pandora said. *And by the way, you should always weigh your choices as to whether they will get you dick or not.*

Can we stop saying "dick" all the time?

Sure! By the way, you should always weigh your choices as to whether they will get you Richard *or not.*

Katie rolled her eyes and headed down to the training center.

Everyone else was already there, sparring in the ring, practicing with weapons, or using the weights. Katie wasn't sure where she wanted to start, so she walked over and grabbed a couple of wooden swords and started to go through the motions in the center of the pit.

She had gotten used to having swords in her hands, and

was able to wield them in a showy but dangerous (to demons) way. She twisted her body, swirling them over her head and kicking her leg out for an extra boost, following the jiujitsu moves Calvin had started teaching her. She wasn't perfect with the moves, but she was really good with the hand motions.

When she was done with the sequence, she dropped to one knee and breathed deeply to center herself. She glanced up at Korbin's office and saw him watching her, which was nothing new for her—but she had never shown anyone what she could do with swords. She stood back up and returned the wooden swords to the holder.

You know, I think I know the perfect weapon for you, Pandora offered. *You need to start training with a quarterstaff, then move up to a double-bladed staff.*

A what?

It's basically a six-foot pole that has spikes on the ends, she explained. *They are really popular in militaristic societies, and have been used for centuries in hand-to-hand combat. The length is ideal, because you never get too close to an enemy.*

And why would I need these? Katie said. When Pandora didn't answer she called, *Hellllooo? Pandora, come back.*

Pandora had gone dark. Katie stood in the middle of the floor with her hands on her hips, thinking about the quarterstaff. She was proficient with all the weapons on the base, so she figured maybe it was a good time to expand her knowledge.

"Hey," Damian said, walking up behind her. "You look like you are deep in thought. Is your demon talking to you?"

"Actually, the opposite." She chuckled. "She went silent

on me, so I guess I should just enjoy it."

"That's probably a good idea." He laughed.

"Hey," she said before he could walk away. "You don't by any chance know how to use a quarterstaff, do you?"

"I haven't heard those words in a long time," Damian said with a chuckle. "You are taking it *way* back old-school."

"Yeah, but sometimes we have to fight old-school, so it's important to be ready for that," she told him.

"Ok, very true." He scratched his chin, thinking. "Unfortunately *I* don't know anything, but go online. I know there are a ton of videos on it."

"Okay." Katie looked at the computer on the table against the wall. "Thanks, I'll do that."

Katie wasn't sure why she was listening to Pandora, especially after she had just dropped off, but she was intrigued.

She walked over and sat down at the computer and put on the headset. She googled Quarterstaffs and found several videos that explained how to fight with them. It didn't look that much different then what she was already doing, and the simplicity of it drew her in.

No one had time for long drawn-out moves during a demon battle, so it needed to be a tactical fighting technique that would improve their kill rate while not putting them in more danger. The Quarterstaff seemed simple and useful, and put a distance between the demon and the wielder. She was pretty impressed.

Now all she had to do was physically maneuver the pole, but she knew that just because it looked easy didn't mean it would be.

For the next two days, Katie spent most of her time researching the quarterstaff and practicing the moves in the training area. She didn't have an actual staff, so she used a six-foot-long, one-inch diameter wooden dowel from Joshua's workroom to practice with. She was starting to get the hang of it.

Damian would come and go, watching Katie and keeping his eyes and ears open for anything else sneaking up on him.

On that day he had something he had to do, and he wasn't sure that it was going to be a pleasant experience. He left the sanctity of his chapel and took a deep breath, then made his way up the stairs to Korbin's office. Their leader was working on the construction designs for the company's building next door.

Damian stood in the doorway and waited until Korbin noticed he was there. He knew his news would put Korbin on high alert, and he hated to do that. The man had enough on his plate as it was.

Korbin finally glanced up. "Oh, I'm sorry. How long have you been standing there?"

Damian chuckled. "Not long. I didn't want to interrupt."

"What's up?" Korbin asked, motioning to the chair.

"I'll stand." He smiled. "I just wanted to let you know that I have to meet with a priest of my order in town, so I might be unreachable for a bit."

"Okay," Korbin said. "Is it something that I should be worried about? Should I put together some back up just in case you need it, or do you need me to be there with you?"

Damian thought about the situation, but figured it would be safer and more efficient if he just went on his own and took care of whatever the problem was. He shook his head. Korbin looked at him for a moment as if he were studying his soul.

"No," Damian said. "I got this one."

"All right," he said, waving him off. "Do what you need to do. If you happen to need us for something, please don't hesitate to pick up your phone and call or text us. We are so close that we could be there in a matter of minutes."

Damian smiled. "I appreciate that. I think I should be more than okay this time, but I will keep my phone close just in case I need anyone's help."

"Good." Korbin sighed. "In the meantime, I'm just going to burn down the place next door so I don't have to design anything else for it."

"Please don't." Damian laughed.

"I'll do my best to practice restraint." Korbin chuckled. "Go ahead and get out of here. I don't want you guys to be out there in the middle of the night if you don't have to be."

"Got it, boss." He saluted him and left.

Katie yawned as she sat up on her bed and put her book down. She didn't want to take another nap because then she would end up not sleeping that night, but she was exhausted from all the work she had been doing on the quarterstaff.

Pandora still hadn't talked to her at all, and it made Katie a bit suspicious.

She stood up and went down to the main area, hoping that someone would do something to help her wake up. She walked through the living room, finding only Jeremy, who was asleep in the reclining chair.

It looked like *everyone* was a bit exhausted from the training they had been doing lately. As she went to leave the room Damian walked in, dressed to leave the base.

Katie smiled at Damian as he walked past, figuring she had no other choice than to give into her tiredness at this point. Damian glanced over his shoulder at Katie, stopping in his tracks and thinking for a moment. He really didn't want to do this thing on his own, and he knew that Katie was not only gifted, but that she had everyone's back. He shrugged and turned around quickly.

"Hey," he called.

"Yeah?" she asked, facing him.

"I have to go meet someone at a church," Damian explained. "I was wondering if you would join me?"

Katie stared at Damian, really not wanting to go to some church meeting with him. She thought about her options: either she went to bed, or she got out of the house and helped her friend. She really couldn't say no. He sounded more timid than she had ever heard him before.

"Okay, sure. Let me just change my clothes really fast."

"All right," he said. "Thank you."

"Of course." She smiled, then jogged back to her room.

Katie went through her clothes, trying to figure out what would be appropriate for a church meeting.

She had never really gone to church, so she wasn't sure what the protocol was.

Finally she just decided to put on her normal black

attire as if she were going on a call, but she carried the vest instead of wearing it. She didn't like to be unprepared. When she was ready, she turned the lights off in her room and headed back out to meet Damian.

"You good to go?" she asked.

"Yeah," he said, obviously lost in his thoughts.

Katie nodded and followed him down to the garage. They got in one of the SUVs, and Damian drove away from the base toward the city. They started to get into the busier part of town, and Katie stared out her window as they passed chapel after chapel.

"This isn't one of the small chapels to get married with Elvis, is it?" she asked, chuckling.

"No." He took a left. "My meeting is with one of the top officials of my church," Damian explained. "He apparently has heard disturbing stories about the Damned from one of his outside contacts. I'm not sure what he is going to tell us, but it seemed important."

"Is his source reliable?" Katie asked. "We don't want to deploy people for something that may be a distraction."

"This priest only deals with people he knows he can trust with these secrets," Damian told her. "I doubt he would have anything to do with crappy sources or people who don't know what they are talking about."

Damian stared straight ahead as he drove toward the church. This guy knew a lot about him, and he almost felt bad at that point for bringing Katie into it.

Still, he couldn't have left without her. He was scared to go alone, and for good reason—there was something in the wind. Something didn't feel right about the whole situation, but he couldn't turn down a request from this fellow priest. They only contacted each other if it was a true emergency and met in secret, and he knew that better than Damian did.

"Do you think this is a good idea?" Katie asked.

"Which part?" he countered.

"Me going in with my red eyes, you meeting a member of the church secretly," she listed. "And the fact that something about this doesn't feel right."

Damian took a deep breath and slowly let it out.

Katie was right; there was a lot of risk involved in what they were doing, but the meeting had become essential to their fight to keep the demons at bay. At first Damian hadn't really thought the whole thing was a good idea, but after he considered it further, he realized that it was the right decision to go—just not for the original reasons.

He looked at Katie and smiled.

"I wouldn't have brought you if I thought it was a bad idea," he told her. "I know that it feels strange and that this is very risky, but it's important that we continue to stick together as a community—at least 'we' as in the rest of the congregation and my fellow clergy. If the priest really does have important information, it may be key to us beating these demons; sending them back to where they came from. It would be really nice to end this war and move on."

She nodded silently. Both knew there was a chance that they wouldn't see the end of it in their lifetimes, at least. They might live and die right there in that town on the edge of nowhere.

Watching the world collapse around them.

7

———————

Damian drove in silence. He seemed more nervous than normal, considering that "normal" was driving toward an operation against demons or spirits.

Or to a bar for a drink.

Katie kept staring out the window as he drove, anxious and surprisingly nervous herself. She assumed it was coming from Damian. His feelings were transferring to her, or perhaps Pandora's were.

She took a deep breath and tried to push it away, something she had been working hard on; especially lately, with the guys constantly being around the house. The combination of feelings and emotions from her teammates was exhausting her.

Damian reached the edge of the Strip and kept going, making a couple of turns and keeping his eyes straight ahead. Katie wondered how far off the beaten track this place was, and hoped that it wasn't too far in case they needed backup later.

After about fifteen minutes and five more turns, Damian slowed down and pulled into the parking lot of a small church.

The building had seen better days. It was missing shingles, had graffiti on one side, and a window in the door leading to the basement was broken. The landscaping was unkempt but manageable, so she assumed some kind of service was still held there on a regular basis.

Like, once a year.

While Damian parked, Katie looked at the door, where four men were waiting on them—or on Damian, at least. One was obviously a simple driver, but he was a big man; probably a foot taller than Katie.

Oh, hell no, Pandora squeaked. *They can sense me, and I don't want that to happen.*

Okay, Katie replied.

She dropped down in Katie as she had done when Damian had first tried to figure out what type of demon she was. She made herself as small and meek as she possibly could, and though Katie knew it was necessary, she didn't like it at all. She felt exposed; unprotected, and downright vulnerable to everyone around her.

Damian came around and helped Katie out of the truck, looking down at her with nervous eyes and back at the church.

"Let me do the talking, okay?" he asked. "This is one of my bosses, who has asked to speak with me."

"No problem," Katie replied. "I never was very good at talking to church people."

"Neither was I," he said with a wink.

"Oh." Katie grabbed Damian's arm and whispered, "I thought you should know that Pandora has made herself look like a little baby demon."

Damian frowned and looked at the group. The men stared back, waiting for them to approach. There was a chill in the air, something Katie hadn't felt before, and between that and Pandora shrinking herself, Katie felt fear of the unknown for the first time in a very long time. She wasn't sure what to expect, but she wasn't going to move a muscle until Damian asked her to.

"Why don't you join me?" he asked. "And do you have backup?"

"Damn right I do," she told him. "Smith & Wessons, but I spell them P-a-n-d-o-r-a—which is pretty much all I need in this world to get past a human or a little demon in human flesh."

"Don't underestimate these men, Katie. I don't know if any are infected, but I do know how powerful they are, Damned or not. This is my archdeacon, but he is also a decisionmaker within the priesthood of my religion. He, like me, was formerly a Jesuit."

"Right." Katie shook her head. "Still, I've got Pandora."

That's right, bitch, Pandora whispered in her mind.

Katie smiled and pulled her leather jacket closed over her red t-shirt and jeans. Beneath her jacket were two pistols; snugly tucked away, but accessible when she needed them. She wasn't going to take any chances. She didn't care if they were part of the church or not.

Not being a religious person, as far as she was concerned they were nothing more than powerful people, and they were upsetting her friend and coworker. It wasn't okay, and she wouldn't stand by and watch for long.

She followed Damian, looking around the parking lot and at the street. The church guys apparently had their backup right there with them. Katie didn't sense or see anyone else in the area, but she could never be too cautious.

Damian's anxiety level had increased, but you couldn't tell by looking at him. He was just as ominous as usual, but with these men he had to force a smile to move across his lips. She knew it was fake, but there was nothing she could do to help him.

Gravel crunched beneath their feet as Katie and Damian approached the front of the church. Damian smiled and put out his arms, hugging the people waiting for them.

He was acting like he was happy to see everyone, but no one looked happy to see Katie.

In fact, she got the feeling that her arrival had not been in the plan, but that was okay. The last thing she wanted was for them to go through whatever plan they had—not without her starting to trust them, which, given the looks on their faces, was not in the cards.

Damian talked to the men, leaving Katie standing there behind him.

She didn't know what else to do at that point, so she smiled brightly. She could feel the pistols pressing against her sides; they would afford her enough protection if she had to act quickly. She felt like she was in a western and had just walked into a strange bar.

"Damian." The archdeacon swept an arm away from the group. "Come talk to us in private."

Damian looked back at Katie and winked before walking over to join them at the top of the stairs. Two of the four church members led Damian toward the grave-yard on the edge of the property, while the third man and the driver stayed with Katie. She didn't like how they were staring at her, as if they were bullying her without words. She smiled at them again, but they just stared at her with blank expressions. Katie could tell they were up to something, but she couldn't figure out what since Pandora was hiding instead of where she needed her to be—which was front and center, ready for action.

Katie shifted uncomfortably, clearing her throat and looking down at the gravel. She scraped the toe of her shoe through the gravel and looked back up at the men standing with her, then took a deep breath and turned toward the driver as she tried to figure out the best way to start a conversation. She had always hated moments like that, where you knew you should talk, but you didn't know what to say.

"It looks like it's going to be another hot day out here," Katie began.

"It does," he replied. "It's a lot drier heat than California though, so I am okay with it."

"Is that where you're from?" Katie asked.

"I lived in San Diego for a while," the driver said.

"It's nice there," Katie replied. "Really beautiful, but expensive as hell."

"That is definitely true." He laughed, but quickly straightened his face when he glanced at the other church member.

Katie tried to keep up the small talk while watching Damian and following their conversation. It had started out just fine, with hugs and smiling. However, as time began to wear down, Katie could see the situation getting dimmer by the second. Damian was no longer smiling, and the archdeacon was asking a barrage of questions. Damian wasn't saying a word, just standing there. After some time spent refusing to answer any questions, he finally gave up and shook his head.

"How dare you!" the archdeacon yelled. "I am your superior, Damian. You *will* obey me, and tell me what I want to know."

"I will do no such thing," Damian snapped back.

"Then you will feel my wrath, and the girl with you shall be the first to go." He chuckled.

Damian narrowed his eyes, staring into the archdeacon's.

She tilted her head, surprised by his expression. Slowly he reached into his trench coat, moving his hand toward the special cross that he carried around with him. Katie unobtrusively started to back away from the two men, realizing that he might be reaching for the cross because the archdeacon had been possessed.

She slid her feet apart and kept her hands tightly at her sides, waiting to react if Damian did what she thought he was going to do. Both men looked at Katie suspiciously, but they had yet to catch onto what was happening.

The air was almost perfectly still around them. Katie could feel her heart beating wildly in her chest.

She couldn't remember a time when she had felt this nervous during an incursion, outside of her first two.

This was different, though. These were men of the cloth, and very important to society. Damian slowly reached forward and grabbed the archdeacon's hand, and pressed his cross into the man's flesh.

It sizzled, and the archdeacon let out a bloodcurdling scream. Katie knew that was the sign to act. She threw a hard right hook, which clipped the driver's jaw. She stood back and he dropped to the ground like a sack of potatoes.

"I'm really sorry." She winced. "But you never leave someone at your back."

The driver groaned as Katie turned to the other church member. The two of them did a little dance, reaching for guns but not shooting yet. She wasn't even sure he had a weapon on him, but she sure as hell did not want to find out if she didn't have to.

Slowly they circled each other, eyeing each other from top to bottom to size up the competition.

When they had turned in a complete circle, the guard lunged forward, trying to take her down. She dodged and pulled out her gun, smacking him hard in the back of the head. He groaned and fell on top of the driver, out cold. Katie winced again, knowing that was going to hurt badly when he finally woke up. As she straightened up, a bullet whizzed past her head.

Katie ducked, and turned to see what was going on with Damian and the other man. Damian was fighting the archdeacon, and the other man had aimed his pistol right at her. She grabbed a knife from her side and threw hard. The guy was thirty yards away, but she hit him squarely in the thigh.

"Don't kill anyone," Damian yelled. "Tie up anyone who is unconscious or hurt. We need them to stay alive for now, and I need you to make smart decisions."

Katie nodded and looked down at her hands. Before she could even think of calling Pandora back into the situation, there was an ear-splitting scream from across the lawn. The guy who'd had the knife thrown into his leg was reacting to the metal, so Katie knew that he too had been infected. He went down a second later.

Damian blocked as the archdeacon's arm crashed down on top of him, knocking him to the ground. Katie's eyes widened as she headed toward him, determined to help him. As she got closer, though, he put up a hand and shook his head.

"This is *my* fight," Damian snarled.

Katie slowed down and finally stopped, understanding how delicate the situation was. She watched as Damian stood back up and growled in anger—not at the archdeacon, but at the demon who had taken his body.

It was obvious to Katie that Damian cared for these people, and that watching them do such terrible things was really hard on him. He moved to the side, letting the archdeacon's arm glide past him before grabbing him by the shoulder and punching him in the gut. Damian's knee rose as the archdeacon's head went down.

Katie winced when the two connected. The archdeacon went down just like his driver had; a giant pile of man on the ground, completely and totally unconscious.

Damian put his hands on his knees and looked at the ground, breathing heavily. All the demon-infested humans were unconscious, but Katie had no idea how long they would stay that way. When Damian had recovered somewhat, Katie went to him.

"We need to get these people tied up and out of harm's way," Damian said. "Go get the rope out of the truck, and we will move them inside the church."

Katie nodded her head and jogged back to the SUV, grabbing the rope from the back and helping Damian carefully carry each of the men into the lobby of the church. Once they were tied up securely, he checked each of them for a demon. Sadly, all were infected.

"I just can't believe that these leaders of our religion could be overcome in their faith," Damian growled, shaking his head. "It makes me so damned sad on so many levels."

"I know." Katie put a hand on his shoulder. "I'm sorry, Damian. I know this must be hard for you."

Two of them have very sneaky demons in them, Pandora explained. *And the third never believed in the first place.*

"Damian, would the archdeacon—the man you know—would he rather be alive with a demon, or dead?" Katie asked.

"I would have thought dead, but now I am not so sure," Damian replied.

"Don't lose faith, Damian." Katie cracked her knuckles. "We don't know the story yet, but we will very soon."

8

K atie watched the men as they began to stir, growling and pulling at the ropes binding them.

Damian stood to the side, not wanting to hurt any of them and trying to figure out a way to get them back without killing them.

These men were important to the church and to Damian personally, and it was his duty to make sure as best as he could that they returned safely to where they had come from. Katie walked toward the archdeacon and squatted in front of him. He growled and snapped at her, his eyes growing larger by the second.

It wasn't anger in his eyes, or even fear. It was *recognition*.

"*You!*" he hissed. "You are a wanted demon, my dear."

"Get in line for your chance to snag her," Katie told him with a smirk.

"You are actually the one I was trying to find for

T'Chezz." He gurgled in laughter. "He wants your pretty little head on a platter."

"Well, it looks like you found me." Katie smirked. "Now what are you going to do?"

Damian stood back and watched Katie's interaction with the archdeacon, trusting that she wasn't going to physically damage him.

She turned to Damian. "Got anything to put in his mouth?"

Damian turned left, then right, not really sure what she was asking for. He reached into a nearby pew and grabbed a small hymnal. He slammed it a couple of times against his leg, and then handed it to her. "This work?"

"Yessss." Katie's voice wasn't entirely her own as she took the small book and turned it so that the spine was toward the archdeacon. She grabbed the man's cheeks and hissed, "Open up!"

She slid the book between his teeth.

Damian's eyes grew large and the hairs stood up on the back of his neck.

A muscular paw came out of her chest, its skin scaly and black and the claws long and sharp. It went into the archdeacon's chest and grasped something inside tightly.

The archdeacon's body began to shake, his eyes rolled back, and foam formed at the corners of his mouth.

Now Damian understood. She didn't want the archdeacon to bite his tongue.

The archdeacon snarled wildly, and although Damian wanted to help, until that demon was removed there was nothing he could do. Katie's eyes grew red as her demon started to pull the archdeacon's demon from his chest.

"Demon," Katie called, her eyes now completely red. "*Sacerdos ex hoc veni! Sacerdos ex hoc veni! Omnia sancta, exímes te!*"

"What are you doing?" Damian yelled.

"I'm trying to coax the demon out so I don't hurt your friend," she explained. "Otherwise this will beat him up so badly that he will wake up wondering what the hell happened to him, with no recollection of a demon invasion."

"Please." Damian's voice was a whisper. "Just help them."

Katie screamed loudly, and her voice echoed through the old church. She needed to pull the demon's attention away from the priest. The paw clenched tighter inside the archdeacon's chest and he groaned loudly, wheezing for air. She knew if she didn't get that demon out of him soon, he was going to die.

"*Sacerdos ex hoc veni! Sacerdos ex hoc veni! Omnia sancta, exímes te!*"

After several attempts, she was able to pull the demon out of the priest's body. As soon as the demon was removed, the priest collapsed and his breathing returning to normal. Katie stood up. The snarling and hissing from the demon apparition in front of her grew loud as she allowed Pandora to speak through her.

"I can make you a delicious deal," Pandora cooed.

"What is that?" He chuckled.

"If I were you, I would keep the laughter to a minimum," Pandora growled. "I will not destroy you completely if you tell me who's trying to find our weapons and stash."

"I will tell you nothing," he growled.

She laughed. "Okay, then I hope you enjoy the fortieth level of hell."

"Wait," he said, becoming very quiet. "There may be someone you know working to find those weapons. Your human let the cat out of the bag in LA, and now T'Chezz wants her head and her swords on a platter. There has been nothing like this in over a thousand years. You think that because you are a Seventy-Two you can just allow it to happen? Even *help* these humans?"

"You are not fighting for our leader," Pandora snapped. "You are fighting for a demon who *thinks* he should be a leader; a demon who will get what is coming to him. If I were you, I would get out before it gets really bad. You know you can see it coming."

"I will only get out of this when you are buried in hell and my leader is standing in his rightful place on top of mounds of human bodies," he growled. "You do not scare me. You are weak and pathetic. You can't even control your human."

Pandora hissed and lifted the demon high into the air, squeezing with a passion unlike anything Damian and Katie had seen to date. Light burst from the demon's chest as she chanted. As wind began to blow through the small church, Damian stood back and covered his head, trying stay out of the path of flying debris.

"*Ad inferos enim tuo tu et daemonium parum est amicitia,*" Pandora hissed. "Back to hell for you, and your little demon friends too!"

As the demon screamed in agony, Pandora burst into a deep maniacal laugh.

There was a bright flash of light, and the demon was gone. The church stilled.

Damian watched in shock as the demon paw retracted back into Katie's chest and she let out a deep breath, cracking her neck back and forth. The archdeacon was slumped over but breathing, and Damian was still in one piece.

There were two more demons to dispose of, but Katie took a moment to gather herself. She was woozy; unlike before, when she had bounced right back.

That demon was stronger than most, Pandora told her. *It takes a lot out of you for something like that, but trust me—it will be easier with these two numbskulls. They think they are badass, but they really are puny little suckling demons.*

Katie shook her head and looked at Damian. The priest was expressionless, just standing there with the cross in his hand. She steadied herself and finished the project, removing the demons from the other two men.

The only one who had not been infected was the driver. Damian agreed to talk to him about what had happened and what to do next, so that he could choose whether to have his mind wiped.

The rest of them would wake up unharmed, with no recollection of what had happened there that day. It had been a success for the most part; no one had been seriously injured, and the infected had been exorcised.

Damian was relieved, and made the sign of the cross when Katie wasn't looking. *Perhaps*, he thought, *you should judge a person by their actions, not their words.*

Katie went over and sat down in one of the pews, staring up at the church's stained-glass windows. The night had passed as they dealt with the demons, and it was well into morning.

Damian was getting the men from the church cleaned up and situated so that their people could come pick them up. Luckily, since they worked for the same ministry as Damian, there was no real explanation needed for what had happened. Katie turned back toward the front of the church and leaned back against the wood. She wasn't a religious person, but she had to admit that the church had a calming effect.

In this place you could really think; process what had happened in your day, and look at your future.

So, while you were sleeping on the couch the other day, Pandora started, *there was a commercial for women telling them to treat themselves to a day at the spa. I was confused by what that meant, since that kind of treatment was reserved for royalty the last time I was on this plane. Apparently it is for every woman now, because the commercial said, "All women are queens."*

Okay. Katie chuckled. *What are you trying to tell me?*

I did a lot of work today. I would like to have a spa day, please, to celebrate the queen in me. It doesn't have to be super-fancy, but you will get enjoyment out of it too. Come on, Mom, pleeeeease?

For the love of God, don't ever call me "Mom" again. Katie put a hand up to her eyes.

Sorry, Pandora replied.

What exactly does this spa you want to go to offer? Katie asked. *There are some spas that offer "services" I won't allow.*

Wait, Pandora said, *you mean like "happy endings?"*

Yes, among other things, Katie replied. *There are some seriously shady places out there, and I don't want to end up goosed when I am least expecting it. I know you have a hyperactive sexual drive, but I don't, and I will not put myself at risk for diseases, pregnancy, or the million other things that can happen when you have sex in a spa.*

Sex? Pandora exclaimed.

Yes, sex, Katie snapped. *What in the world did you mean by "happy endings?"*

I don't know—you get married or something, she explained. *I didn't know you humans got all freaky-deaky inside massage parlors*

I feel like somehow I just made the whole situation much worse for myself. Katie sighed. *I should have just asked for the name of the spa and been done with it, but no! I ran my mouth, and now my demon is going to go look for massage parlors where she thinks she can get it on.*

I mean, it does sound tempting, Pandora replied. *If I had my own body, I would love to go to a place like that—though I have a feeling that it is better for a man than a woman in one of those places.*

Probably, Katie grumbled.

This is so cute. Pandora chuckled. *And someday, maybe, but no. I want a full day of soaps, gameshows, and donuts, not necessarily in that order.*

Really? Katie asked.

I mean, yeah. Those are my three new favorite things and I have to beg for them, so if I can get them all at one time I will be golden, Pandora told her. *I can already imagine how amazing it will be, curled up in a blanket, eating donuts, and watching the* old creepy guy on the soap opera marry the rich twenty-year-old. There is so much wrong with that, it titillates my gazoongas.

I don't know. Katie thought for a moment. *That actually sounds nauseating.*

Maybe you are right. Humans and their weak stomachs, Pandora grumped. *We can do the donuts after that episode. Maybe we can even get dinner somewhere that night, just the two of us.*

I am going on a date with my demon? Katie laughed. *This is how pathetic my life has turned out to be. My family thinks I am dead, and I am dating my demon. Wait, the fact that I even* have *a demon is a testament to my shitty-ass luck. I wasn't a goth or a vampire. I liked Star Wars and was going to school for a degree in business, but somehow I morphed into this demon-killing crazy bitch. I don't even know what is going on anymore.*

Are you having a breakdown in a church? Pandora asked. *From what I've heard, Jesus can save your ass.*

Right. Katie shook her head. *I think he might be a bit miffed with me at the moment.*

Hey, if I were you, I wouldn't count anything out. Pandora chuckled. *Sasquatch, Nessie, Jesus...the list goes on and on.*

Maybe you are right. Katie sighed. *I'll look into heaven's side in the future.*

Let's ignore that last part and get back to my spa day, Pandora said. *Is that a yes?*

I suppose so, Katie replied. *It actually sounds like a really good time right about now. And you know what I'll do?*

What? Sleep with someone? Pandora asked excitedly. Katie could almost imagine that vivacious lady she had seen in the coven's circle jumping up and down, her damned perky breasts too strong for gravity as she clapped in excitement.

Uh, no, Katie replied. *But I* will *get you a donut that you will never forget. Something super-amazing.*

I like what you are cooking up here, Pandora said. *Special donuts, soaps, gameshows, dick—it all sounds perfect.*

Wait! I never agreed to dick, Katie said in a menacing voice.

I know. Pandora sighed. *But a girl has to at least give it a shot, right?*

I suppose, Katie agreed. *But you will never win that one.*

I wouldn't say never if I were you, Pandora replied. *One day you might wake up with a hankering for some penis. Just sayin'.*

Can we maybe not talk about cock when we are sitting in a church? Katie requested.

Oh, yeah. He sees you when you're sleeping, he knows when you're awake, Pandora sang.

Katie laughed. *That's Santa Claus, not Jesus.*

Same freaking difference, Pandora told her. *They are both creeping on you right now.*

You want me to see if Big J will have a talk with you?

Oh, no, Pandora bitched. *My confession would take years, and he's too bright to look at. I'd need shades.*

You need help—like professional help, Katie commented, looking around as some of Damian's church people filed in with stretchers and medical bags.

They got each of the priests onto a stretcher and quickly carried them out of the church. Damian followed them to the front door and then turned around, staring at the mess all around them.

He smiled at Katie as she pulled herself off the bench and walked over to him. She looked around the room in silence, shaking her head. The wind had blown things everywhere.

"I guess we should start cleaning things up," Katie declared. "I'll take the right side, you take the left, and we'll meet in the middle."

"Works for me," Damian agreed.

Katie walked through the pews picking up pages from their choir's hymnals and broken glass from the light bulbs that had exploded during the exorcism, and pushing the benches back where they were supposed to be.

The only thing different—and much nicer—was that this fight had ended without a single dead body. They could just walk away free and clear. Just then Katie's phone buzzed in her pocket and she pulled it out and opened it up.

"Hello?" Katie said.

"Elizabeth, this is Brian. I wanted you to know that your car is here, and it's clean, gassed up, and ready to go!"

"That is amazing news, and perfect timing." Katie sighed, a happy smile playing across her face. "You are officially the hero of my day!"

9

W hen they finally pulled up back at the base, both Katie and Damian were exhausted. They'd had their fair share of excitement for the day, and were not looking forward to the debriefing with Korbin.

Korbin'd had no idea that there would be trouble at that meeting, even though Damian had a little bit of an inkling that there would be. Nonetheless, they would have to report to him on what had happened, and what they were told by the demon that had infected the archdeacon.

Katie decided right then and there that demon-infested priests were exceptionally scary, except Damian—you couldn't even tell with him.

They walked inside and headed straight to Korbin's office, not wanting to waste any time.

When they got to the office he was on the phone getting the financial report, surprised to see that Damian and Katie had earned some money earlier that day. They had both hoped they would get there before he got that call. When he hung up, he motioned for them to come in and sit down.

"So." He steepled his fingers in front of him and eyed them. "What in the world happened?"

Katie was resolute in her courage, and she turned to Damian to tell the story.

"My archdeacon and several other priests were infected by some rather nasty demons," Damian admitted. "The main one had information about T'Chezz and the fight for Earth, and was very powerful and nasty."

"Really?" Korbin exclaimed. "Was he one of the Seventy-Two?"

"No," Katie told him. "And he wasn't particularly high on the totem pole, either. He was fairly easy to exorcise. Well, anything would seem easy after the mammoth T'Chezz sent up after us in San Diego and LA. This one was maybe a few levels above the normal everyday demon."

"That's so strange," Korbin mused. "Maybe he thought something a bit less conspicuous could get him closer?"

"Maybe." Katie glanced at Damian. "Also, he was looking for the weapons."

"What?" Korbin's eyes opened wide. "We are *not* ready."

Katie nodded. "Well, we had to see that coming. We used them on that monster demon in California not once, but twice. T'Chezz had to realize by the end that something big was going on up here."

"True." Korbin reached behind his ear to scratch an itch. "I was just really hoping that we would have a bit more time. I wasn't expecting them to come down on us quite yet."

"Me either," Damian agreed. "But I'm glad the priests are okay and that everyone got out of this one alive."

"Except the demons, of course," Katie replied.

"All right, come on." Korbin stood up. "Let's go check out the tunnel and make sure everything is straight."

The three of them headed downstairs to the training area, went through to the weapons room, and came to a stop in front of a large wooden bookshelf. Korbin pulled three books forward halfway until the lock clicked and the bookcase swung open to reveal a passageway.

The underground tunnel led into Joshua's workspace. It was the easiest and safest way to get in and out of there without putting yourself in danger by going through the front door. Joshua had already retired to his new room in the basement and they didn't want to bother him, so they headed up to the ground floor. When they reached the top of the steps, though, all three of them stopped and stared at the flimsy wooden door separating the two spaces.

"Well, this is going to do absolutely nothing if we get attacked," Katie said. "A strong breeze could blow this thing open."

"Yeah," Korbin said. "We need to replace this door with one made of reinforced steel—thick, like a vault door — and we could have it lock with a combination so only people who know that combination can come and go."

Katie chuckled. "I feel like we are locking Joshua up in a cave."

"We kind of are, but it's definitely for his own good," Korbin said. "Those demons are after the weapons, but they are also after the person who knows how to make them. Joshua is the only one left with that knowledge.

They would snatch him up in a heartbeat, and either use him for their own amusement or kill him on the spot."

"That's... Well, fuck." Katie's fist squeezed tight, guilt running through her for dragging Joshua into it. "I feel terrible. He is such a good guy, and now he is going to be hunted."

"They have *all* been hunted," Joshua said from behind them. "They were all hunted from the moment they took the magic into their hands. *That* is the destiny of my family. Everyone knows that as soon as they make that first sword, they are destined to be hunted for the rest of time. It is just what it is. There is no feeling bad about it or even being scared of it. Most of my family didn't have a group like you protecting them. I think my dad somehow sent you guys to me because he knew I struggled with protecting myself."

"Aw." Katie stepped over to wrap her arms around him. "You are one of a kind, and I love you so much!"

"Love you too." He laughed, a little less tense now. "I didn't say that to get your attention, though. I said it so you understand that a strong door would be great, but what's even better than that is having the courage to stand up and take whatever they throw at me. I'm not afraid of them. In fact, I'd love to have the chance to put my sword through one of their bellies. They killed my father, who was part of a team. One day I'll have my revenge, but for now I just want to get as many weapons made as possible."

"And you will." Katie stepped back, her eyes flashing. "You will."

When they were done touring the building and making sure that they took note of everything they had to fix to make it safer, Korbin went back to his office, Damian went to lie down, and Katie headed up to see what Jeremy and Eric were doing. She walked into the living room and grinned at them both.

"Hey there, smiley!" Eric laughed. "What's up?"

"Nothin' much," she replied. "What are you guys doing?"

"We are going to Area 51," Jeremy told her excitedly. "We figured, we've never been there and we are so close, so why not?"

"Wow," Katie exclaimed, shaking her head. "That was *not* the answer I expected."

"You wanna come?" Eric asked, closing his backpack.

"Uhhh, no, thanks." She smiled. "I was actually wondering if you could drop me off at Bootlegger on your way out."

"More Italian food?" Eric shook his head. "I heard that monster last time."

Katie laughed. "The key is portion control. And this time I'm going to have some drinks, so I don't want to drive."

"Yeah, sure, come on. Let's get going." Eric waved her toward the door.

"Yay!" Katie skipped behind them.

During the whole ride to Bootlegger Jeremy talked about Area 51, and though things like that would normally interest Katie, she was focused on something a little bit shinier. Her car was ready, and she was ready for it—and had been for quite some time.

She just wanted to pick it up and hit the road for a little while with the top down.

"All right," Eric declared, "here we are!"

Eric pulled into the parking lot of Bootlegger Italian Bistro and Katie climbed out of the car. She walked up to Jeremy's window and leaned against it, looking at his excited face. She chuckled a bit and tapped the side of the truck.

"Well, you boys have a good time. Don't get abducted or arrested please."

Jeremy laughed. "No alien in their right mind would want to abduct demon-ridden humans."

"Hey, they might not know!" Katie replied. "You might spread your demons, and accidently start an intergalactic war."

"We will do our best to avoid that." Eric waved. "Have fun with your food."

"I always do," she told him, stepping back.

She waved as they drove out of the parking lot and disappeared down the street, then pulled her phone out of her pocket and hit the Uber app to schedule a pickup. She leaned against the light post, eager to go pick up her car.

I can't believe we are going on Uber again, Pandora griped. *That shit is a bait-and-switch, like last time when there was that hot guy who only wanted other hot guys.*

Aw. Katie laughed. *Maybe we'll get lucky this time.*

Yeah, right. She scoffed.

"So," Jeremy asked, looking out the window as they sped

toward the diner near Area 51. "What do you think about all of this? I mean the demon-hunting."

"I love it," Eric told him. "Though I have to be honest: my attachment to Korbin is not quite as deep as the others'. I think I will work with Korbin's group for a couple of years, then maybe transfer to another team because...well, deserts aren't really my thing. Don't get me wrong... There is definitely a beautiful quality about the desert, but I'd prefer the trees of the upper Northwest, like Seattle."

"Nice area," Jeremy agreed. "I've never been, but I've heard it's gorgeous."

"I mean, I'm happy enough here," Eric continued. "I'm not *un*happy, that's for sure. I don't want to leave Katie for a little while, since she helped get me infected."

"Your infection is the reason? Or is it that hot body?" Jeremy teased.

Eric looked at Jeremy. He was sitting there laughing, pretty proud of himself for that comment. What he didn't realize, though, was that Eric didn't find it even remotely funny. Eric shook his head and looked back at the road.

"So, do you think that there are actually aliens connected with Area 51?" Eric asked, changing the subject.

"Nah." Jeremy shrugged. "It's fun to think about, but I think it's just a super-secretive Air Force base that handles new technologies and stuff."

Eric sighed. "I agree. I think it's just secret weapons and such."

"I do think it's shitty, how they treated those people that owned Groom Lake Mines," Jeremy said. "They came in, offered them an absurdly low number more than once, then just seized the lands. There was no time given for them to vacate, either. They appropriated their personal property, then tried to say the place was only worth three hundred thousand when the appraiser estimated closer to a hundred million."

"I know, but it was a matter of national security," Eric replied. "We have to keep that base secure. It rather sucks that now technology is so good that you can see Groom Lake from the mine, even though it's pretty far away."

"Yeah, but what about the price?" Jeremy repeated. "They said it was worth three hundred thousand, but first offered the family $1.2 million. After the family had it appraised for $44 million, the Air Force offered $5 million. Of course they refused."

"Yeah, but part of that $44 million was distress over burial grounds and equipment," Eric shot back.

"Personally, I think it's the government being fucking greedy," Jeremy declared. "They didn't give a rat's ass about those people. They wanted to give them pennies on the dollar for that land and all their equipment, and when they said no, that's not fair, they snatched it right out from under their noses. That's greed, man."

"Maybe they were greedy, or maybe it wasn't as black and white as it seems." Eric shrugged. "I don't know...it all seems a little crazy to me that the family, knowing the government would seize the land and they wouldn't get anything, didn't take the offer."

"Would you take an offer for forty million less than something was worth?" Jeremy asked.

"I don't know," Eric replied. "Guess I would have to talk to my family; make it a joint decision."

"Did you have anyone back at home when you decided to join?" Jeremy asked.

"Nah, man. I mean, I knew not to do that," Eric said. "I wanted to join, but I knew I couldn't have any loose ends. I made sure to stay as far away from relationships as I could. I had some one-night stands in there, but no one I even took a number from. How about you?"

"Yeah." He sighed. "I had a pretty solid relationship with someone, and I was even looking at rings when I got my demon. She was the first person I thought about when it happened, you know? I was heartbroken, I won't lie. I had the rest of my life with her planned out. She was my best friend, even if it does sound hokey."

"Nah." Eric shook his head. "Not hokey, truthful. I like that. Do you ever check up on her?"

"Honestly, yeah." He shrugged. "I have, a couple of times. I try not to do it all the time, though."

"How is she doing?" Eric asked.

"She seems like she has gotten past the rough part; the initial shock and mourning," Jeremy replied. "I mean, at least the FBI claimed I was killed—which gave her some closure, you know? It didn't leave her wondering if I was still out there. It doesn't look like she's hooked up with anyone else so far, either."

"God, I would hope not! It hasn't been that long," Eric said.

Jeremy shrugged. "I wouldn't have thought she would either, but then again, I never thought I would have a demon inside me. Things definitely have a way of changing up on you when you least expect them to. It's a struggle for me, for sure...no bullshit. But I know that my girl is still out there living her life—being beautiful, being strong—and that makes a hell of a lot of difference to me, you know? It makes me want to work harder to protect her, even if I'll never get to see her again. I love her."

"Good for you," Eric exclaimed, watching the desert as they sped past. "Love is what keeps it all together in the end."

10

"Oh my God, I know," the Uber driver said. "Boys are so gross. So why am I taking you to the Ferrari dealership?"

"My car just came in!" Katie exclaimed in excitement.

"Oh my *GAAHHHD*," she replied. "You bought a Ferrari?"

Katie snickered. "I sure did."

"What in the world do you do for a living?" the driver asked.

"Um, I'm in universal securities," Katie said, unsure if that even made sense.

"I don't know what that is, but crap! I'm in the wrong business," the driver replied with a snort. "Okay, here we are! Congrats on the new car! That is so exciting!"

"Thank you," Katie said, running a debit card and tipping her. "I'll keep your card, though, just in case I don't feel like driving."

"Do it!" the driver said enthusiastically.

Katie got out of the car and waved at the Uber driver as she drove away. Katie hadn't actually thought about the fact that she missed having women in her life until that moment. She really did, though. She missed having girlfriends; people who understood life as a woman.

Hey, you have me. Pandora snapped.

Right, and you are inside me, Katie shot back. *And you aren't really up to speed with this century and the shit that we go through.*

You're right. Pandora sighed. *And I don't like humans anyways. By the way, that girl is false advertising. She was wearing ripped black clothes, black lipstick, and she had bright green hair and dark eye makeup. She seemed like the kind of girl I would seriously have something in common with. I mean, she looked like one of Satan's followers...*

Pandora grunted. *And then BOOM! She fucking talks.*

Katie laughed. *What was wrong with the way she talked?*

She was just so damn human, Pandora grumped. *She gave a shit about what people thought of her, and she gushed over a goddamn puppy for like ten minutes. Seriously, I would have bitten the head off her puppy and not felt the least remorse.*

You scare me sometimes, Katie said as she walked into the dealership.

"Elizabeth," Brian said, smiling across the room. "It's the big day!"

And this *fucking guy...* Pandora scoffed.

Be nice. He still has the keys to the car, Katie said, smiling back and waving.

"So, are you ready to see your new beauty?" Brian asked.

"More than ready," Katie replied.

"Well, let's go then."

Katie followed Brian out to the back lot and stopped, her mouth falling open. There it was...freshly painted, spotless, and with a pretty red bow across the windshield. Katie smiled and ran to Brian, giving him a huge hug.

"*OH*." He laughed. "Elizabeth, thank you so much for coming out here to pick your car up. Do you want me to get your phone synced in or anything?"

Katie shook her head vehemently. "I just want to get in and drive!"

Brian smiled. "OK, but please call me if there are any issues or you have questions at all."

"I will," Katie said, taking the keys from him and winking. "Thank you so much."

"It was my pleasure." Brian waved her to the car. "Now go! It's all yours!"

Katie giggled and skipped over to the car, pulling open the door and taking in a huge whiff of the new-car smell.

The top was already down which was fine with her. She sat down in the driver's seat and groaned, rolling her eyes.

This was *her* new baby; she didn't have to share it with a single person. It was the first new car she had ever owned, and she had to admit she had splurged quite a bit, considering it was worth more than her mother's house.

But she had the money and she had the stressful job and the boxed-in life, so it was a release—something they all needed from time to time. All she had to do at that point was figure out where to drive first.

Derek grabbed his file and headed down the stairs toward Korbin's office.

He had been trying a new experiment where he put up a website with some information on it and waited for people to start commenting and talking, hoping he could get some clues on who was demonic and what people were saying about the most recent events.

It wasn't something that cost a lot of money, but it did cost time. He wanted to make sure he and Korbin were on the same page before he moved forward with more sites.

When he got to the office the door was cracked, so he peeked his head in and saw that Korbin was on the phone. He looked up at Derek and waved him in, giving him the sign for one minute. Derek nodded and wandered around the office, looking at all the books on his bookshelf.

The man was definitely a collector, which was really nice to see. Those things tended to get lost in their world. After a few minutes, Korbin got off the phone and let out a long sigh.

"Sorry about that." He stood up. "Please, have a seat."

"The higher-ups giving you a hard time again?" Derek asked as he sat.

"No, not really. They just have to go over every minute detail, and it's exhausting," Korbin griped. "I wish they would just put it in a memo that I won't read and go from there."

Derek laughed. "That's probably why they don't."

Korbin sat down behind his desk. "So how is the whole thing going? The webpage thing?"

"Well, it has borne a little fruit already," Derek said, "but mostly it has produced a huge number of false positives. I fully expected that, but it is a little frustrating at times—I'm not going to lie. I want to scream at the computer at least ten times a day."

"So what kind of false positives are you finding on there?" Korbin asked.

"It's people who either live in another world, or they think the website is like a fantasy fiction kind of thing," Derek explained. "For example, I had to delete like a hundred comments that had nothing to do with what we were looking for, but everything to do with Dungeons and Dragons. They get on a roll on there, and there is just no stopping them. If I don't delete their comments anyone legit who comes to the site just will pass it over, thinking we are full of shit or made everything up. They won't see their connection to it all."

"Right," Korbin agreed.

"Oh, and I had to delete a ton of comic-book characters like Spawn and Dead Pool," Derek continued. "They were comic relief, and though I appreciated it, I am taking this very seriously. This is our future, you know? At this time and place we are facing something no one has ever seen in their lives. It is historical...and terrifying at the same time. I want people to start taking it seriously, or at least attempt to. I am just surprised that I didn't get any *Cards of Humanity* fiends! Go figure. You attract one kind of nerd and repel another—just great."

"You are moving forward though, right?" Korbin asked.

"An inch at a time." Derek sighed. "Sometimes just a centimeter at a time, but forward is forward, I guess."

"That is true, and we knew it wouldn't work overnight,"

Korbin assured him. "So, among all the bullshit, is there any useful new intel?"

"I mean, not really." Derek shrugged. "It is all still pretty evenly distributed across the country, to be honest."

"That's okay," Korbin replied. "It's just the beginning, and none of us expected this thing to be the save-all. You have to remember that all these things contribute to the bigger picture. A little intel from you, a little intel from the reporter, and we are putting pieces together before we know it. It takes time; that's something I learned in the service. *Everything* takes time, especially when you need it right then and there. There's no easy solution, unfortunately. Every once in a while you get a good tip and it's magic, but most of the time it's sifting through the shit before you find that one piece of gold."

Derek raised an eyebrow. "I appreciate the pep talk."

"Well, that's what I'm here for—the professional pep talker." Korbin laughed. "I should charge for it, but then all of you would be broke and complaining."

"That is very true."

"So, tell me what else you think you could do to push the site out of fantasy fiction and more into underground news?" Korbin asked.

"Put up stories or articles, maybe," Derek suggested. "Something to drive people there and start them thinking about what they have seen or done, you know?"

"That's interesting, but you don't want it to take up all of your time," Korbin warned. "You want to be able to put up the pertinent things and have it run itself, almost. You go in, check for intel, post something else, move on."

"That's true," Derek agreed, making a note on his tablet.

"Also, you could add in some murder stats and connect them to additional databases to run some information," Korbin offered. "You could get the statistics going—the pure data. People love numbers, whether they are lottery jackpots or murder rates. This will get them to start thinking, right?"

"That's...a really interesting idea," Derek mused, writing it down. "I'm not positive about how to connect those things, but I'm sure with a little bit of research I will have it down in no time."

"See?" Korbin smiled. "You sit there day in and day out going over the numbers, but you start to lose focus when it is like that. Sometimes it takes stepping away from the screen and going over things with someone else—me, or any of the other people in this house. We are lucky enough to have a solid group of smart people. People who can think outside the box. They are strong-willed and strong-minded and educated and experienced, and you have them at your fingertips. All you gotta do is grab someone and say 'Hey, give me five minutes.'"

"Right," Derek agreed, feeling better already.

"Oh, and I suggest that you ask James Caplan to come out of retirement," Korbin told him. "He has done some stellar consulting work for me in the past, and you can trust him fully. The biggest issue is figuring out whether we can actually get him."

"All we can do is try," Derek replied. "I mean, it's not going to hurt. The worst he can say is no, and we haven't lost anything with that. My mom always told me it never hurt to ask."

"She was very right...unless it's a stupid question."

Korbin chuckled. "I don't agree that there are no stupid questions."

"Why does that not surprise me?" Derek asked, still making notes.

"All right." Korbin rubbed his hands together. "I give you my approval to reach out to James, but be very vague on what we need at first. Once he hears my name he will understand why it needs to be vague, especially over the phone. He will come in if he is interested, and we can give him a better rundown of what we are trying to achieve and where we want to take this project."

"Awesome," Derek exclaimed, standing up and shaking Korbin's hand. "I'll check back in with you later this week."

"Sounds good," Korbin agreed.

Derek felt better about his project when he left the office, and headed down to the main area.

Once he got there, he decided he needed a break; some time to just clear his mind. He headed up on the roof with his tablet.

Rarely did anyone go up there, so it was the perfect place to be alone and uninterrupted.

Everyone else was perfectly okay with being up each other's butts, but not Derek. He cherished his alone-time. That was when he did the stupid shit most people made fun of him for.

He plopped down on the lounge and turned on his tablet, then went to his social media and scrolling through the lives of people that he didn't know at all but had friended to make his account look real.

From there, he followed his normal routine of scanning through the memes of the day in several different groups that he belonged to. They were stupid but funny, and funny was a perfect break from the stress of the life he led.

His life consisted of constant doom and gloom, constant death, constant attacks, constant dark alleys, and constant blood baths, so if he could sit back for a couple of hours and laugh at llama or cat or even Ryan Reynolds memes, he was all about it. It was what he had done before he came into Korbin's Killers. Before he was part of the Damned, before he knew demons really existed.

It made no difference to him that his life outside of that was different. He just focused on the laughs.

After about an hour, he looked up from his tablet and set it in his lap.

The sky was bright blue, and the breeze was almost hot as it rolled over the desert. He closed his eyes and thought about a life without killing.

He thought about the family he would never have, the house he would never buy, and the car he would never own.

He thought about his prospects for a future outside Korbin's Killers, but what would he do? Sit on a beach, drink mango juice, and drum on a goatskin bongo? Nah, that wasn't him. He had to be needed. To be important, and vital to the world's functionality.

He wasn't positive about the last one, but he sure as hell was *trying* to be vital, and the website was going to help him get there. He knew he could create a tool to help with the fights. He just needed to figure out the answer to the question at the back end of the code; the missing link that would tie it all together.

He just needed the final puzzle piece.

11

Mamacita sat at her desk and stared down at the books. There were plenty of calculations to be done, and this was the first time that she'd had time to sit down and do them. She was tired of rushing through them right before the ordering, so she had now made it her rule that she would get them done at least one day before ordering. That way no matter who was there or who did the ordering, everything was set up for success.

Before she could begin, though, Joshua walked into the office.

"Hey!" He grinned at her. "I wanted to ask you a couple of questions about quotas and exchanges."

Mamacita smiled. "Well, look who is all business *now*! Please sit down."

"Thank you."

"Why now?" Mamacita asked. "Let me rephrase that: why the *interest* now?"

"Well, I have to admit that in the beginning all I wanted to do was be left alone to make my weapons," he told her. "I liked the quiet and the solace, and I didn't want to have to deal with customers or anything. Of course, I would have failed miserably if I hadn't, but I was unhappy and anxiety-ridden the whole time. Now, though, it's different. I see the help that the others are giving me, giving you, and giving the company. I want to be a part of that, beyond just hammering out weapons. And most importantly, I don't want to fail for a lot of reasons, but mostly because I know I can do better than I have until now."

Mamacita listened to him with her hands in her lap and her face calm. She considered his words, his tone, his body language, and the story he was telling beneath it all.

She waited until he was done, and paused for a moment to think about what she wanted to say to him. She knew that with Joshua you had to be specific. You had to be on-point, but in a personal way.

You had to connect with him on his level.

"Let me ask you a question," she began. "Who do you think the highest-level business people are, as far as careers?"

"I-I-I don't know. Maybe bankers?" he suggested.

"That's a good guess, but no," she told him. "The highest-level business people are either engineers or in sales. They are working together, but they are on the same level in business."

"How are they working together?" Joshua asked.

She smiled. "Well, think about it. You have the one who created it, and then you have the one who sells it. Engineers usually hire someone to work the business side, because that isn't where their talents lie. Like you: you are very knowledgeable about creating the product. That is your expertise, and no one can even come close to doing your job. Then you have me and Korbin, who are really good with the books, so we focus all our energy there. We may be interested in learning how you do what you do, but we will still be better at the books. You are irreplaceable, though, and that makes you the most important man in this entire building. You push harder than anyone, and you are responsible for making the product that we will be selling."

"Oh, okay." Joshua nodded. "You are saying, stick with your strengths. Learn your weaknesses, but operate where you are the strongest."

"Yes," Mamacita agreed.

"So, like Katie—she helped get the business on track, but she was overwhelmed in the beginning," Joshua said. "You and Korbin have a lot more experience on the business side, so you are taking over that part—at least for now —to make sure the company runs smoothly—so you aren't having to dump money into it all the time because of bad deals with suppliers. Also, you are making sure that when I have done my job, you have a home for the product. It's like a circle where we want the strongest people we can have at each point, so that we stay strong all the way through from beginning to end."

"You got it." Mamacita smiled, a glint of pride in her eyes. "You are even smarter than you give yourself credit for. You understand complexity in such a unique way, and it's wonderful and refreshing. Now, I do want to point out that just because Katie didn't know what to do, it doesn't mean she was a bad owner. She reached out. In fact, being willing to reach out for help even when you are at the top is a very big indicator that you are a leader."

"I've always wanted to be a leader, but it's really hard because I get so nervous, and sometimes I get confused," Joshua admitted.

"And that's okay, because guess what? You are the leader in your *specialty*," Mamacita told him. "Just like Korbin and I are leaders in ours. You are the boss of the weapons."

"I think I know what I need to do, then," he said, closing his notebook. "Instead of focusing on something I'm not good at, I should be perfecting what I do best."

"That's a very good way to look at it," Mamacita agreed. "And what is your plan?"

"Well, I think what I want to do is talk to Katie about finding more help to get the production up," he replied. "Of course, that would depend on whether the girls are interested in having more work here, or more hours doing this instead of their other jobs. They are the only ones that would be allowed in the building, so I would have to come up with another idea if they aren't interested. Maybe someone from the team, but I doubt it."

"I would be more than happy to speak to the girls on your behalf," Mamacita responded. "I just want you to remember that most of these girls have scraped by since Day One of their little lives, and while they love being here and getting a break from their other work, some of them are in it strictly for the money. Unfortunately, knowing the books, you wouldn't be able to afford to pay some of them enough to leave their other job. It isn't personal. If they were given the freedom and money didn't matter, they would almost all choose to work here with all these wonderful people—and you, whom they all adore. Unfortunately the world isn't always a fair place, so we make do. Just like you have in the past—sleeping in your van and doing the best you could."

Joshua stood up. "Thank you, Mamacita. You have helped me, at least to understand this better."

The wind blew through Katie's hair as she cruised along the boulevard, taking in the scenery, feeling her own car beneath her, and actually enjoying the attention she was getting for once. Everyone loved the car, and it was pretty obvious that they thought the girl in it was smoking hot too. Katie admitted it was going straight to her head. She hadn't had attention like that in a long time. In fact, she didn't know if she'd ever experienced attention like this before.

I love this interior, Pandora gushed. *It's gorgeous! It's color-coordinated, and it is really comfortable to sit on. Seriously, the last time I rode in any kind of vehicle-type-thing it was a carriage, and let me tell you...those carriages in Rome, they were not comfortable in the least. Even when I rode with the finest ladies of Rome, the pillows didn't keep my ass from getting sore. It was horrible most of the time.*

Damn! What was Rome like? Katie asked.

Smelly, hot, and there were breasts hanging out everywhere, she replied. *But all in all it was really beautiful, what with the* grapes and the wrath and the murder. It was juicier than our soap opera, that's for damn sure.

Katie wrinkled her nose. *That sounds horrible!*

Maybe for a human, but for me it was heaven, Pandora replied. *The carriages, they only had one advantage over these tiny little cars, and that was space. You could, if the road was not too bumpy, enjoy yourself physically in a carriage in olden times. Whether you were all alone taking care of your business or with others, there was enough room to bend forward, backward, grab your ankles—whatever he preferred.*

You are the worst, Katie grumped. *Seriously, you should be focusing on the positives, and instead you are telling raunchy sex stories for kicks and to get a rise out of me.*

Oh, honey, Pandora replied. *You are giving yourself way too much credit. I am just reminiscing, not trying to get a rise out of you. Maybe the guys in the barracks, but not you.*

Katie sighed. *Okay, go on...I want to hear all about Rome. Was it the way it is in movies?*

Actually, yes. They have done a respectable job in most of the movies you have shown me of depicting what the scenery was like, where people lived, and how they dressed. They have done an amazing job with it, in fact. The only thing I can say is, women mostly wore dresses and these shawls called "pallas," not togas...even the poorer women. Men wore togas on a daily basis, but the extremely poor people wore these tunic things. But any woman with her name on the Roman's lips, she wore some sort of beautiful dress, lots of them imported. I, of course, wore all the latest fashions, and could woo just about any man I wanted while I was there. It was one of my favorite periods in history.

Did you take many lovers in Rome? Katie asked.

Oh, look at you, asking the right question! Pandora snickered. *The answer to that is yes. Those Romans, they sure knew how to do a woman right. They were so strong, so manly, and the way their bodies glistened in the firelight was fantastic. And that Nero...oh my, did he know how to blow off some steam!"*

Wait, Nero, as in the Emperor Nero? Katie asked. *The emperor who was Claudius' heir and reigned over Rome until his death in 68 A.D.?*

You know your history, don't you? Pandora laughed. *Yes, that Nero.* Emperor *Nero.*

Did you have anything to do with how despicable Nero was? Katie asked.

Nero was a master of his time. A child of the Roman chaos, Pandora told her.

Right, so did you have anything to do with his murders, his debauchery, or his persecution of Christians?

He had learned his hate at an early age. He was too naïve to understand the world around him but too pig-headed to slow down and learn, so he made a lot of mistakes. But I will make it clear that no matter how much he liked music, he was in no way a fiddler.

What's wrong with fiddlers? Katie asked. *And you are dodging my questions. Did you have anything to do with his suicide, then?*

Let me just be clear on something, Pandora continued, dodging the question. *Nero was his own special brand of wrong all by himself. He didn't need me or anyone else to move him along.*

You did *have something to do with it, didn't you?* Katie gasped.

Did you know that I spent a brief bit of time in this country right after Columbus sailed the ocean blue?

You mean when he came onto native territory and shot and murdered over thirty people, and that was just him? Katie asked.

Well, you have your own viewpoint on the settlement, Pandora said. *Though I have to say, you are pretty up on our political view of history.*

It isn't political, Katie snapped, irritation rising. *It's the truth, unguarded and unfiltered. It is what the schools should be teaching, but instead they celebrate Christopher Columbus and pretend like historical events never happened."*

"*Are there still Indians?*" Pandora asked.

"*A ton,*" Katie said. "*But we call them natives or indigenous people or First Nations people now. Or you can call them by their tribe name, which they usually give out when introducing themselves. Our government gave them tiny bits of land and they made do with what they had, but we still treat them terribly today.*

Leave it to the human race to be even more despicable than the demons sometimes, Pandora muttered. *I can still see those pioneers, as they called them, shooting the Indians right in the face.*

Anyway, Katie continued, *I can tell that you don't want to talk about Nero and your part in his torture and murder of dozens of people, but how can you sleep with someone who took someone else's lives in rage like that?*

I am a demon, Katie, Pandora answered in an even tone. *You forgot that again.*

Yeah, yeah. Katie sighed.

Katie made a right turn and drove as fast as she could through an alley, hoping that no one walked in front of her.

She really wanted to open up the new car and feel that adrenaline rush, but she figured she would just wait until she could get out in the desert or something like that. In the meantime, it was about time for her to start heading back to the base.

She'd had a big day, and she couldn't wait to wow everyone with her new car. Hopefully Korbin didn't completely lose his shit with her, though.

Even though it was dangerous, Charlotte was secretly having a blast doing undercover work for Korbin and his team.

She felt like a real reporter, and for once she believed she was actually doing something worthwhile, not just providing idiot readers with tabloid headlines to fuel their conspiracy obsessions.

She was looking for a real bad guy, and attempting to get enough information to nail him for whatever atrocities he was bringing into the world.

That night she dressed carefully, not wearing one of her normal underground outfits. She didn't put on excessive makeup, nor lace up her black calf-height boots. Instead she wore a nice dress, blue and white, with her hair down her back with little ringlets at the bottom, and she spritzed herself with the perfume her mother had given her three Christmases before that was still in the box.

She left her apartment and drove to Hollywood,

parking a couple of blocks away from the bar since her car wasn't the most glamorous thing. She walked to the corner right next to the bar the politician frequented, and stood there pretending to window-shop. As soon as his car pulled up out front she scooted inside, grabbing a seat at the bar and ordering a martini for looks.

In reality she hated martinis, but shots of whiskey wouldn't fit in with her look that night. She glanced up nonchalantly as the politician walked past, completely ignoring her.

"Best way to not be caught trailing someone," she muttered under her breath, "is be in front of him, waiting like a spider."

She took the small cocktail straw from her drink and sucked on it, wincing slightly at the bite of gin in the back of her throat.

She turned slightly on her stool and crossed her legs, looking up at the television but keeping the politician in her peripheral vision. He walked to a table away from the bar, and three men dressed in expensive black suits stood and shook his hand. The first man was younger, probably around Charlotte's age, with black hair slicked to his head and large rings like her rich old uncle had worn when she was a kid. His smile was fake, and you could see the malice in his eyes.

The second man was middle-aged, short and round, balding, and he carried a pocket handkerchief in his right hand to blot the sweat from his brow. He smiled nervously, and didn't look the politician in the eyes. He was shifty, with remnants of his lunch on his white button-up. The buttons strained across his belly.

The third man looked like the boss of the group—mid-forties, and his face was stern like a father chastising his son. He was very clean cut, and very business-like. He looked the politician in the eye, shook his hand coolly, and was the last to have a seat at the table.

The waitress quickly brought drinks over, bowing her head as if she were afraid they would eat her right there in the middle of the bar. The middle-aged man slapped the waitress on the ass, and chuckled as she jumped and scampered off with tears in her eyes.

It was obvious he came there a lot and was not a staff favorite, but he had money—and in that town, and probably every other town in the country, money talked.

Anti-harassment legislation didn't always make it down to the street-level.

The men leaned in and started talking and Charlotte slowly shifted toward them, trying to aim herself in their direction without being caught. She strained her ears, but she couldn't figure out what they were talking about.

"Is your drink okay, miss?" the bartender asked, startling Charlotte.

"Oh, yes. It's wonderful, thank you," Charlotte told the man as she looked at her drink and up at him. "I'm just so into this...this...uh, hockey game."

She looked up at the television, realizing what she was staring at, and nervously laughed. He raised both eyebrows before throwing his towel over his arm and walking away.

He wasn't part of it, she could tell, but now he thought she was neurotic.

Maybe she was. She shrugged and picked an olive out of her drink, popping it into her mouth as she glanced over at the table. The round man pulled an envelope from his jacket's inside pocket and handed it to the leader of the group, who proffered the envelope to the politician. He said something as he held it out, but Charlotte could only make out the words, "this is it." He put the envelope down on the table and tapped his finger on it before standing up and buttoning his jacket.

Charlotte turned back toward the bar as the other two stood, followed by the politician. The leader of the three men threw some cash down on the table and shook the politician's hand, smiling. The politician hadn't changed his blank expression the entire time he was there.

Charlotte turned her head away as the men left the table and dispersed, walking out the front door and then all in different directions. The politician got back into his car, and it sped off. Charlotte looked back at the table and saw the envelope sitting there.

She paid the bartender and walked toward the bathroom in the back, nonchalantly grabbing the envelope from the table and slipping it into her purse.

When she was alone and hiding in a bathroom stall, she pulled the card from the envelope and read it. It was an invitation to an exclusive event in Las Vegas for VIPs, with gambling, an open bar, and a very exclusive party at the end. It was not really a scene for a low-level politician, but knowing what else he was into, this party just might be his next hit.

Charlotte shoved the card in her purse and left, wanting to get the information back to Calvin, Katie, and the others.

Fast.

Derek, Calvin, Eric, and Jeremy were all lounging in the main area, recovering from their day's shenanigans. Jeremy was reading a book about Area 51 he had picked up, Eric was watching some cooking show on the television, Calvin was eating, as usual, and Derek was slumped in his chair flipping through his phone, occasionally chuckling at some stupid picture he found. The evening was relaxed, everyone decompressing and readying themselves for another training day in the morning.

"Where is Katie?" Damian asked as he entered the main area.

"I don't know," Jeremy replied. "Last we saw her, we dropped her off at Bootlegger before heading to Area 51, but that was earlier today. We haven't heard from her since."

"Oh, lord," Damian said, rolling his eyes. "They are probably rolling the girl out of the restaurant at this point."

"I'll text her." Calvin switched to his messaging app, chuckling. "Maybe shake her out of her food coma."

Calvin typed a text, but before he could send it, everyone heard a car engine revving. Damian walked over to the window and glanced out, and a smile moved across his lips. He shook his head and looked back at the gang.

"I found her." Damian chuckled, pointing out the window. "You guys might want to see this."

One by one the guys looked out the window and then ran for the door, taking the stairs two at a time until they reached the door to the outside. Katie laughed when the door slammed open and the guys piled out, oohing and awing at the sleek design of her California T.

They circled the car, reaching toward it but afraid to touch it. She turned off the engine and hopped out, walking over to Damian.

"Wow, that's a nice ride," he told her, nodding. "I don't think they sell those at Bootlegger, though."

She laughed. "No, I ordered it last week."

"You ordered what last week?" Korbin asked as he walked up to them.

"That," Katie said, nodding to her new car.

"Whoa!" Korbin exclaimed, staring from the Ferrari to Katie with an eyebrow raised. "How in the world did you pull *that* off?"

"Just like *that*." Katie snapped her fingers.

"It's, uh, pretty sweet," Korbin agreed. "But seriously, how did you pull it off?"

"I got a fake identity—which is actually not fake, just not my original one—and I paid cash at the dealership," she explained.

Korbin slapped his hand over his eyes and shook his head. Katie could tell he wasn't too happy, but at the same time he wasn't making a big deal about it. He took it in stride, which was different for him. He uncovered his eyes and looked at the guys, who were all drooling over the car.

He finally laughed. "That is really awesome. It's a beautiful car, but I think you unleashed a monster."

"What monster?" Katie asked, pulling her brows together.

Korbin pointed at Eric.

"Envy," he said, moving his finger to Jeremy. "And lust."

Oh, I like this! Right up my alley, Pandora cooed. *Those are good ones. Had I known this would happen I would have helped a shit-ton more.*

It is not that bad, Katie replied. *This is just boys being boys. There's something about a nice car that makes them drool. I don't get it—though I am starting to understand with this car—but it is like embedded in guys' DNA.*

Now you are sounding more like me, Pandora quipped. *"Boys will be boys." That they will, and I freaking love every second of it.*

You are so carnal, Katie griped. *Seriously, you don't do anything without thinking about sex first, or at least the opposite sex. You need to start being comfortable in your own demon skin so you can take or leave a man.*

What is this heresy you prattle of? the demon replied dryly. *Who would leave men behind? I mean, they are such beautiful creatures. Even these idiots have worth to them; the kind of worth that would leave me exhausted afterward.*

All righty, I guess this conversation is lost on you. Katie laughed. *Maybe we will try again in a couple of months.*

Mmmhmm, Pandora murmured. *Or you will finally see it my way and drop this fem obsession.*

It is not an obsession! Katie exclaimed. *It's a truth, but I know the truth hurts sometimes. It's okay. One day you will ease into it, and you will see why I am so much stronger on my own.*

Yeah, but you are a grumpy bitch, Pandora snapped. *And I know a little wang in your thang would relax you quite a bit. Maybe you would even smile.*

Smiling causes wrinkles, Katie replied.

I don't even have anything to say to that, Pandora told her.

Good, now we can get back to our day, Katie shot back with a smirk.

After about two hours of the guys gawking at the car, Katie pulled it into the garage and put the top up. She figured that if she had to leave in a hurry, she would rather have it up than down in the rain.

Like it ever rained in Vegas. This damned area had two settings: none, and *"oh my God, it's the end times!"*

The guys were so pumped up. They were wildly reminiscing about their first cars, places they had been, their childhoods, and everything else a little nostalgia could stir up in them.

Katie knew Korbin wasn't thrilled at what she had done, but he could see the lift it had given the guys. They were alive, they were on-point, and they were in high spirits for the first time in what felt a really long time.

It was a nice thing, she decided, no matter what Korbin thought.

Everyone went inside and sat down in the living room, still talking and laughing. Katie went back to her room to put away her stuff and decompress for a few moments.

It had been an exciting day, and she was tired from that excitement. She sat down on the edge of the bed and laid back, putting her arms under her head. She closed her eyes and relaxed her body, feeling the sleepiness start to creep over her. Just as she was on the edge of slumber the alarm went off, the red light flashing wildly over her door. She rolled right out of the bed and rubbed her face to push away the fatigue.

"Attention! This is not a drill. Please dress for combat and report to the training area immediately," Korbin ordered over the speaker.

Katie threw off her clothes and pulled out a fresh pair of black leather pants, a tank top, her jacket, socks, and boots, and got dressed as fast as she could. She had not been expecting to go on a call that day, but that was the nature of the beast.

She pulled her hair back in a ponytail and looked at herself in the mirror as she pushed her knives into the holsters on her vest. She opened her drawer and grabbed her two pistols, checking the clips and then pushing them into her belt holsters. She grabbed her earpiece and jogged out of her room, pushing it into her ear as she made her way to the elevator.

When she got to the training area, it was only her and Damian.

Korbin walked out to address the team and stopped, putting his hands out as the guys meandered into the room. Katie glanced at Damian and back at Korbin, standing straight and ready.

"By all means, ladies—no offense, Katie—move at a glacial pace," Korbin snarked as they lined up. "All right, here is the deal: the incursion is in Henderson, not far from here. As usual we have limited intel, but they will be updating us when we get on the road. So, pack up and let's head out."

Korbin clapped his hands and the team dispersed, moving quicker now toward the SUVs. Katie opened the back of one of them and started to load the equipment. Jeremy walked up to help, grabbing duffel bags and throwing them in.

"You're not going to drive your new car to the op?" he asked.

"Seriously?" She looked at him like he was crazy. "You mean take my very expensive, fucking hard-to-purchase and *brand-new* car to a location where shit gets destroyed? Are you out of your fucking mind?"

"They keep telling me I am." Jeremy chuckled as he tossed in another bag.

W hen the SUVs were all loaded, Katie jumped
in with Damian, Eric, and Calvin and they
sped off behind Korbin, Jeremy, and Derek.
Everybody was silent as they tried to get into the mood it
took to walk into an incursion. The moments leading up to
the call had been fun and light-hearted, and it was really
difficult to just switch over like that—especially when such
days were few and far between for the team.

Katie wouldn't have taken it back, though. They had
been normal for an afternoon, and that was worth its
weight in gold to her.

As they drove the team put their earpieces in, waiting
for Korbin to give them further instructions. They really
had no idea what they were walking into, except that the
area was really rich. It was known as "The Hills," and
looked down on Vegas from a distance. It was a beautiful
view, with the lights of the city in one direction and the
rolling desert in the other.

People had to have serious money to live there. It didn't surprise Katie at all that there was an incursion in one of the homes, though. That kind of place held at least some immoral and unethical rich people.

She just hoped that they didn't come across any huge demons like the last time. She had just started to feel better, and she knew Calvin wasn't one hundred percent yet, for all he boasted about his regenerative powers.

Katie looked at Calvin, who appeared to be nervous. He was leaning forward with his elbows on his knees, palms pressed together, looking at the floor. She wondered what he was thinking, and how he was feeling about going back out there for the first time since the cemetery. She wished there was something she could do to help him get his confidence back.

"You all right?" Katie asked, reaching over and touching him on the arm.

"Yeah," he said, slowly looking up at Katie. "Just giving my demon a little pep talk, that's all."

Katie smiled. "Is it working? Because if not, I know someone who could bitch-slap him around a bit," She paused for a moment. "Literally."

I fucking resent that...however true it is.

He laughed. "I don't think that will be necessary. He is already a bit more talkative, just by you mentioning that option. If he chooses to back down...well, then we will revisit it."

Calvin winked at Katie and she smiled at what he was doing there.

These demons did not want to fuck with Pandora. They would go against everything in their beings to avoid dealing with her. It was actually a pretty good perk of being infected by her…or with her.

Katie never had to worry about dealing with the lesser demons. They wouldn't come near her anymore. In reality, it had kind of taken away the one fun thing about her job—fighting the smaller demons.

She turned back and looked out the window, wondering what they would find when they arrived. She really hoped it wasn't a blood bath like the ones in the recent past.

The SUVs began to slow down, and pulled to the side of the road before stopping. Korbin climbed out, and motioned for the rest of them to join him.

When they were all standing in a circle around Korbin, he pointed to the right at a really nice house situated by itself in the hills. It overlooked Vegas, and was obviously owned by some really rich people.

"That is our target," Korbin began. "The new intel says it was a bit of a bloodbath. There was some kind of party going on when the demons broke through. People are scattered, some inside the house and some outside. We have to eliminate all threats, and from the sound of it there are quite a few, although no large demons have been reported. It looks like we will be dealing with low-level demons, mostly encased in their human hosts. Remember, if there are any Damned you believe can be saved or used for science purposes, please restrain but don't injure them."

"And if they can't?" Eric asked.

"Then kill them right then and there," Korbin stated. "Don't risk your life or the lives of your teammates by trying to be the hero."

Eric nodded. "Understood."

"Now, we are going to split up into two groups of three, with Derek staying behind in the SUV to run tactical," Korbin continued. "The first group will be Damian, Katie, and Eric. The three of you will go into the house and clean it up. The second group will be Calvin, Jeremy, and me, and we will be going out into the desert around the property to collect demon heads from those areas. As always, we will most likely come upon human casualties, though I have been told there are no children this time. There was a party going on; a fundraising event, so there were quite a few people there during the attack. From what we know right now, there isn't a lot of movement anymore inside the house. I am Team Lead for Team Two and Damian will be leading Team One. I want both teams to break out and talk for a minute about strategy. Damian, there is a blueprint of the house in the back of your SUV. As always, good luck."

The teams split up, getting into separate SUVs. Korbin climbed into his, with Calvin at the wheel. Calvin looked at Korbin and nodded, then glanced in the rearview mirror at Jeremy. The man was breathing heavily, but looked ready to go. Calvin winced slightly as he shifted his shoulders, still not completely healed.

"I want you to tell me honestly if you are up for this or not," Korbin told Calvin. "There is no shame in not being healed enough to go into battle. I would rather have you in top shape ready to fight than lose you for some stupid reason like needing rest but being too macho to admit it."

"I'm good to go," Calvin told him, looking straight

ahead. "I'm ready to get back into this game and kick some demon ass."

"All right." Korbin patted him on the shoulder. "Now, when we arrive we are going to pull up the driveway and park, but as soon as we get out I want it to be *go*. There is a brick border around the whole property, which is mostly sand, cactus, etc. We will split up, and Calvin and I will go right. Jeremy, you go left. Check all bodies to make sure there are no survivors, and take down any demon bastards you find. If you need backup, click the button on your earpiece and give your location. We will get to you as soon as our feet can carry us there. Are there any questions?"

"No, sir," Jeremy declared.

"Not a one," Calvin replied.

"Okay, good." Korbin turned back around in his seat. "Then let's get this show on the road. I want to be home in time for dinner."

"That's what I'm talking about." Calvin laughed, shifting the car into drive and speeding off toward the house.

When they reached the front gate they slowed down, swerving between the bodies along the way. There were quite a few dead lying on the grounds, and there was smoke coming from one side of the enormous columned house. Calvin pumped his brakes, seeing flashes of red eyes in the distance.

Korbin put up his hand and Calvin turned, parking to the side of the drive.

"All right, boys, let's get 'em good," Korbin said.

They waited until Damian's team had driven to the front of the house before piling out of the SUV and taking off in their respective directions. The demons scattered, and Calvin counted at least six of them on the ground. He looked at Jeremy as he crept in the other direction, then knelt behind a bush next to Korbin. They peeked around it, watching one demon drag a dead human body to the side, growling and snarling as it ripped into the woman's flesh.

"That caviar-infused body lotion ain't gonna do shit for that rich bitch anymore," Calvin whispered.

Korbin looked at him. "I have an idea. You ever play games like *Duck Hunt*?"

Calvin chuckled. "Yeah."

"I'm gonna creep up the side and push the demons out of hiding," he explained. "When they step into the open, shoot them square in the head with that rifle you got. Sound good?"

"Works for me, boss," he said, knowing Korbin was only doing that to keep things light for him.

Korbin nodded and pulled out his pistols, checking out the side of the house before making a run for it. He pressed his back against the house and shinnied along, rattling the bushes as he went. Two demons suddenly ran out ahead of him, and Calvin took aim. Slowly he breathed out and pulled the trigger, shooting one of the demons in the neck. The other panicked, not knowing where the shot had come from, and ran straight toward Calvin, giving him a clean shot right between the eyes. Both demons fell into a pile on the ground, and their bodies slowly morphed back into the humans they had taken over.

Calvin smiled, and looked up fast at the sound of a twig cracking. Straight down the side of the sandy yard, a demon was creeping around a potted bush. Calvin steadied his rifle and looked through the sight, letting out another long deep breath before pulling the trigger. Korbin laughed, watching the demon writhe and growl until its body turned to dust. Just then two demons darted from behind the house, tackling Korbin to the ground. He pulled his pistol up and shot one of the demons in the head, before the other knocked the pistol from his hand and pinned his arms to the ground. Calvin moved the rifle back and forth to try to get a good shot, but with Korbin struggling it was too risky.

"Lay flat," Calvin yelled.

Korbin released his muscles and laid flat on the ground. As soon as his body cleared the shot Calvin took it, hitting the demon in the side of the head. Korbin wrinkled his nose and spat out demon blood, pushing the dead body off himself before it turned to dust. He looked at Calvin and gave him a thumbs-up.

Calvin pointed the rifle at the ground, pulled out another clip, and slotted it in after removing the empty one.

He chuckled and shook his head, freezing as he felt the hot breath of a demon on his neck. He set the gun on the ground and slowly turned around, staring straight into the beast's eyes. Calvin reached for his knife, but before he could grab it the demon pounced, pushing Calvin down onto his back. Calvin was powerless to move; it had all happened so fast. He could hear Korbin's voice in slow motion as the beast pulled his arm back to strike. Calvin closed his eyes and waited for the pain—for the end—but it never came.

When he heard a gurgle he opened his eyes and stared up at the demon, who was holding his throat, his eyes wide. As his body began to go limp Jeremy tossed it to the side, looking somewhat the worse for wear. His eyes were dark, his lip was bleeding, and he had sand all over him. He panted as he reached down to help Calvin to his feet.

"Thanks, man," Calvin said, shaking his head. "I thought that was really the end, I'm not going to lie."

"You all right?" Korbin asked as he jogged up. "Good work, Jeremy. What happened?"

"You guys…" He paused to try to catch his breath. "You didn't answer the comm."

"My earpiece fell out when those bastards tackled me," Korbin told him.

"I guess mine isn't working." Calvin tapped it. "Are you okay? How many were there?"

"Four." Jeremy was still panting hard. "Four vicious dirty motherfuckers, and I ran out of ammo."

"Shit!" Calvin exclaimed. "And you took all four on your own?"

"Yeah." He chuckled. "And I don't want to do that again. One got me pretty damn good."

Jeremy turned and showed his upper arm, where a deep gash bled hard through a rip in his shirt. Korbin ripped open the shirt to look at the laceration, and Jeremy winced as Korbin pushed on the skin.

"He really did a number," Korbin agreed. "But I don't have time to stitch you up right now."

As Korbin ripped a strip of fabric from the bottom of his shirt and tied it around the wound, Calvin turned and looked at the house; he could see flashes from gunfire inside. Team One had found demons.

"Did the other team say anything on the comm?" Calvin asked.

"No." Jeremy groaned as Korbin pulled the fabric tighter. "Not a peep."

"Should we go in?" Calvin put his rifle on his back and pulled out his short sword.

"Not yet," Korbin told them. "We'll let them do their thing. With our earpieces not working, we could easily be injured by friendly fire. Jeremy, I want you to listen. Keep listening, and if you hear anything from the other team about needing help or someone going down, I want you to tell me immediately. We won't leave them hanging."

14

Katie climbed back into the SUV and waited for Damian, Eric, and Derek to situate themselves. Derek pulled out a blueprint of the house and handed it to Damian, who spread it out on the dash. The place was big but pretty open, which was good—there wouldn't be that many hiding places for the demons to scurry off to. Damian pulled out a pen and made three big circles on the map.

"Okay, this is how we are going to work it," Damian started. "Eric, when we go in, you and I are going to head straight up the main staircase to the second floor. When we reach the top, I will go left, and you go right. Katie, you have the entire bottom floor including the garage, which looks pretty big."

"Got it." Katie looked at the blueprint.

"The bedrooms will be the worst danger zones, so make sure to use your mirrors to check inside rather than just blowing into a room," Damian said. "Katie, you have six large rooms to check, but the only one that looks like there will be a lot of places to hide is the office on the ground level. Take the big rooms first. Work your way from one side to the other so that you know nothing will be sneaking up behind you."

"Right," Katie agreed.

"Eric, just kill the demons. No questions," Damian ordered.

"Katie...well, use your judgment, but don't be a hero," he declared. "If you can save a life, fine, but if not take them out."

Katie nodded. "You don't have to tell me twice."

"Everyone, make sure to have your earpieces in and on. I don't want there to be any miscommunication," Damian instructed. "If a demon gets away from one of us, we need to let Katie know so she can be on the lookout for it."

"Got it," Eric confirmed, nodding.

"All right, guys, let's make this quick and painless, I want to be home for dinner." Damian smiled.

Yes, dinner, Pandora replied.

Don't start, Katie warned.

They drove off after Korbin and the others had already made their way to the house. They passed the SUV, which had pulled into the grass in front of the house. Katie had her pistol in one hand, and her knife in the other. Damian looked back at her and nodded before getting out of the car. Katie looked at Eric.

"I'll be okay," he assured her. "Just keep your earpiece on.

Katie nodded and got out of the car, crouching as she moved up to the front door. Damian grabbed the handle and looked at Katie, who had her gun at the ready. Quickly, he pushed open the door and lifted his weapon. Katie peered into the grand entry, but saw and heard nothing—though her demon senses were tingling.

They cleared the foyer and looked at each other. Damian nodded to Eric and then Katie, and she stood watch as they slowly made their way up the grand staircase and split at the top, one going right and the other left.

Eric crept slowly down the hallway, pulling out his mirror and bending it around each of the open doors. He cleared every bedroom one at a time, but didn't find anything.

When he reached the last door at the very end of the hall, he stopped and listened to a strange sound from inside. It was like muffled snarling, so he knew there had to be some kind of demon involved. He reached for the door handle and took a deep breath, then flung it open and raised his gun. He peered over his weapon with disgust and awe on his face. The demon was standing facing him, holding one of the victim's heads and chewing on its cheek. The thing didn't even stop when Eric walked in, which threw him off.

He shook his head and let out a deep breath, firing three shots into the demon through the human head. He flinched as blood sprayed all over his face. He wiped his eyes and looked down at the demon's body on the floor, which writhed for a moment before turning to dust. Eric shook his head, not quite used to seeing crazy shit like that, and left the room, closing the door behind him. As he stepped forward, not really paying attention, a body dropped onto him from the ceiling and he crashed through one of the bedroom doors. Eric rolled across the floor, groaning, and came to a stop at the foot of the bed.

He shook his head and blinked at the demon, this one licking its lips and crawling toward him on all fours. Eric reached for his gun, but realized he had dropped it when he went flying.

The beast snarled, then a grin moving across its black scaly lips. Eric panicked as the beast moved toward him.

When the demon's face was just inches from his, it licked his cheek. He slid his hand down to his belt, grabbing the handle of his knife.

He slowly pulled it out, waiting for the right moment. The demon didn't notice, just leaned its head back and opened its mouth wide to reveal row upon row of sharp, jagged teeth.

"Get in there, fucker!" As it lunged Eric shoved his knife up through the beast's chin, pushing hard until it pierced its brain.

The demon fell backward and Eric stood, moving to the side, breathing hard with fear.

The demon got to its hooves and yanked the knife from its chin, staring at Eric a moment before dropping it on the floor. He glanced at the knife, then collapsed.

Eric watched as the demon transformed back into its human form, now lifeless on the black Persian rug. He stared down at the body of a young woman not much older than eighteen. His heart swelled, and he shook his head, unable to speak. He sat down on the edge of the bed.

This wasn't what he had expected at all.

Damian slunk through the halls in a crouch, looking for any sign of demon presence. All the doors were shut, and slowly he cleared the rooms. When he was done, he stood in the hallway looking perplexed.

He hadn't found a single demon; not one. He figured that maybe they had all ended up in another area, or possibly even outside. He started to walk forward and stopped, hearing scraping noises above him. He slowly looked up, but there was nothing there. He stood silently, listening for the sound again. When he was about to give up he heard it, like nails, or claws dragging along the wood floors above him. He turned back toward the end of the hallway and noticed a string hanging from the ceiling. It was the entrance to the attic, and there was light shining around the edges of the door.

"Of course." Damian groaned. "Just my luck."

He walked over to the string and stood back, giving it a yank. The door opened, and a ladder tumbled down, forcing Damian to jump back farther, and he fell. He put his hand over his heart and breathed heavily, startled.

After he had gathered himself again, he pulled himself up and began to climb the ladder, cross in one hand and short sword in the other. He reached the opening and made the sign of the cross before entering.

Quickly he levered up, pushing half his body through the opening and looking around. He didn't see anything unusual, just the normal dustiness of an old attic. He had just turned his head to look to the right when a demon popped out of who-knew-where to hiss in his face. Damian yelled and pushed his cross into the demon's face, which resulted in wails and its skin sizzling.

Or was that him wailing? Nope, he was a badass demon hunter, and badass demon hunters did not wail.

The demon fell forward onto Damian, pushing them both down the ladder and to the hall floor. Damian landed with a thump, the demon still on top of him. He groaned, pushing the beast off him, wincing at the condition of its face where the cross had burned off the flesh.

When he leaned forward to see if he could tell if there was a life force still inside, the demon's eyes blew open and he lunged toward the priest, sinking its teeth into his shoulder. Damian screamed, throwing the demon off him and slashing his sword through the air. It made contact with its neck, and the body dropped as the head rolled down the hallway, coming to a stop right at the top of the stairs. Damian leaned back against the wall, closing his eyes and breathing heavily. He looked at his shoulder, where necrosis was starting to spread from the bite.

Damian pulled a purple sash from his bag and wrapped it around the wound, shaking his head in disbelief. Slowly he climbed back up the ladder and lifted himself inside, looking around at the mess. He walked around a few boxes that had bloody footprints on them. As he looked down he groaned, pulling the handkerchief from his pocket and holding it over his nose and mouth. There were two bodies up there, and they were not in good shape. Damian mumbled a prayer and pulled the sawed-off shotgun from beneath his coat. Slowly he made his way back down the ladder and looked down at the ashes left by the demon who had bitten him.

His area was clear, but he had a serious issue with his shoulder to figure out. He had never been bitten by a demon before, just scratched by the claws or wrestled to the ground.

He groaned again, pulling himself away from the wall. He had heard gunshots in the distance, so he knew that Eric was facing his own demons. He could only hope his team came out better than he felt at that moment.

Katie crept through the house, checking the rooms one at a time.

There was no sign of demons in the living room or the large formal dining room, so she made her way to the kitchen. As she opened the door she gasped, finding the ravaged bodies of the staff who had been working the party.

There was something smoking in the oven, so she ran over and turned it off. She pulled open the door and waving her hand through the smoke to clear it. She put her hands on the center island and dropped her head, sad at the loss of so many souls. However, as she stood there, she sensed a demon coming up behind her. Slowly she bent her knees and then leapt into the air, twisting her body and landing on top of the counter facing the demon.

"It's not nice to sneak up on people," Katie said, pulling out her sword. "You don't want to lose your head, now do you?"

Can we exorcise? Katie asked Pandora.

No, they are all too far gone, Pandora told her. *Chop their fucking heads off.*

You got it, Katie replied.

As soon as Katie turned back, she noticed this demon wasn't alone. Four more demons gathered around slowly, circling the island. Katie tapped her sword on the marble top and stood up tall.

"Oh, so you brought your friends too." Katie smirked. "The more the merrier, I suppose."

The demons stopped in their tracks, growling and snarling at her. Pandora boosted Katie to give her strength and agility beyond what she normally possessed.

As the demons lunged toward her she jumped into the air, swiping her sword downward and catching one of them in the back. It screamed in agony and fell backward into the dishes. Katie landed to the side of the island on the floor, and as she balanced her body to stay upright from the drop she pulled out her second sword, slashing both outward from her body and chopping the heads off two of the other demons.

Katie sheathed one sword and pulled her pistol out, aiming at the one she had initially injured and pulling the trigger. The beast went down hard, turning to ash before it hit the floor. She blew on the end of her pistol and turned back around, staring at the last two demons. They watched her with wide eyes.

"Hey, boys," she called as they turned and started to run. "Aw, where ya goin'? The fun was just getting started!"

Katie hopped the counter and sprinted after the demons, running her ass off.

When she caught up with them they stared at her, shocked at how fast she could move. She smiled, pulling her sword back out and swiping it at their legs. One demon fell, tripping the other and sending him flying into the wall. Katie came to a screeching halt and laughed, then walked over to the one on the floor. She raised her sword high into the air and pushed it quickly through its neck. When that one had turned to dust she looked over at the other, who was bloodied and battered from the fall.

"Man, that looks like it hurts," She tsked. "Here, let me make it better."

She pulled out her pistol and fired straight into his head, watching his body shudder before evaporating before her. She smiled as she wiped her swords off and sheathed them.

At least this time they hadn't all run from her.

Korbin went over to the DEA agent as the rest of his team piled into the cars. He needed to make sure that they were on the same page with everything.

The agent smiled at Korbin. "Good to see you again," she said, shaking his hand.

"You too," he replied. "I just wanted to make sure we saw eye to eye. We can't let anyone know we were here, since it would compromise a covert action we have undertaken in search of whoever is behind this recent rash of attacks."

"Yep, we're on it," she said. "I swear, the fucking rich… all they do is take up space and make my life more of a problem than it has to be. And heaven forbid a rich one dies, much less over a hundred. There is going to be some serious political ass-kicking. That never happens when it's a normal Joe Shmoe."

"I don't envy you," Korbin said, shaking her hand again.

"Yeah, yeah," She sighed and shooed him away. "Go on get out of here. We'll handle it all."

She watched as Korbin nodded and climbed into the SUV. She didn't know what was going on, but she knew that if the Killers had been there it was serious.

Things were getting worse in Vegas, and she had a feeling it wouldn't let up anytime soon.

15

The teams headed home, grateful that the incursion was over and no one really sustained much of an injury except Damian. He, however, was obviously playing off the pain he was in.

As Eric saw to his wounds, Korbin explained exactly what he needed to do to neutralize the poison from the demon's bite. Damian had been lucky, but Katie couldn't help but feel like there was something else going on in his head, besides relief.

He looked disconcerted; shaken even, and so did Eric. While Katie had been out there cutting off heads and laughing, her teammates had suffered through what had just happened—and it took her until they were on the way back for her to notice. She felt horrible for it, like she needed to say something to them.

"You guys did an amazing job today," Katie said, watching Eric as he tended to Damian. "Really, you went above and beyond."

"Yeah." Damian scoffed. "One little demon got the best of me."

"I'm right there with you, man," Eric admitted. "Only I had two. When the second demon changed back into its human form, I realized it was just a girl. *Just a teenage girl.* When I took this position, telling myself day and night that I wanted to be on these teams, I didn't prepare myself for something like that."

"Could you ever really prepare for that?" Damian asked. "Seeing someone who was still a child, really…their whole life gone in the blink of a demon eye. It never gets easier when they are so young. I'm sorry that you had to see that. But you can talk to me about it when we get back, or our team therapist, who takes appointments at any time and knows exactly what we do."

"It was bound to happen eventually," Eric replied. "I was just lucky enough to see it at the end, not in the middle of a battle. It could have gotten really hairy if I had gotten distracted like that when I was fighting a demon. It was a close enough call for me tonight."

Katie sat back and listened to them talk. She had started the conversation, but Damian had done a good job taking over, making Eric understand that this kind of thing was pretty normal for their lives—which was really sad.

When they got back to the base, they unloaded their gear and headed to their rooms to get cleaned up. Everyone had blood on them, so the hot showers were a welcome relief.

When they had all cleaned up, they met back in the main room.

Jeremy expressed his need to crash, as did Calvin, and Korbin had wandered back to his office, as always. Damian looked at Katie, Derek, and Eric, rubbing his hands together and smirking. Katie furrowed her brow and chuckled, knowing he was up to something. She just wasn't sure what that something was yet.

"So, are you guys hungry?" he asked.

Yes. Pandora scoffed. *As if the question was necessary!*

Katie just nodded her head while the guys answered fervently. Apparently everyone, including Pandora, had worked up an appetite.

"All right, cool," Damian said. "Come on, let's jump in the SUV. I know the perfect spot."

Katie shrugged and followed the guys out to the truck. She sat quietly as Derek and Eric talked about food, thinking about everything that had gone on that day. She knew Pandora was picky about food, but at that moment she really didn't care. She just wanted to get something into her stomach.

Damian pulled up in front of Herbs & Rye, a very popular joint off Sahara. Inside, the restaurant and bar looked like some sort of twenties pub. The walls were red-striped and something like velvet, and the place was quite narrow. They walked past the bearded bartender, who was wearing a vest and dress shirt, looking like someone from a hundred years ago.

"This place has awesome steaks," Damian said. "And even better than that, it's their Happy Hour, which means their steaks are half-off right now."

Katie looked at the different options on the menu. Not only did they have normal-sized steaks, but they also had party steaks—slabs of meat that a normal person couldn't possibly finish on their own, unless they were Katie with a demon metabolizing her food. She smiled, trying to block the information from Pandora, but it was impossible.

Now that *is what I'm talking about,* Pandora declared. *Eat like a man. Those huge steaks are right up my alley. We need to show these boys the ropes.*

I think that's a bad idea, Katie said. *A really horrible idea.*

Nonsense! They want to eat big? Well, so do we, Pandora replied.

"Who wants to challenge me to a steak-eating contest?" Eric asked. "I am telling you right now, you don't stand a chance against the meat-eating maestro."

Katie smirked, knowing he would fold in a second next to her. She could eat this place out of stock, so she knew there was no way he could keep up. She didn't want to embarrass him.

But damn...how could she turn down a challenge like that?

"I'm ready to go," She closed her menu with a laugh. "Let's do this."

That's my girl! Pandora said. *Let's show 'em who's boss.*

Everyone ordered the biggest steaks, and when they got there they started to chow down.

Katie took her time, savoring every bite as she went through the motions without even breaking a sweat.

Eric was all about it at first, laughing and smiling as he plowed through his meat. Then it hit him, and with every bite Katie could see his resolve fading.

After Eric took his last bite he was clearly in pain from all that meat; it showed on his face. She smiled as his mouth slid around that last piece of beef, and she waited until they were dead tied before taking just one more bite than him.

Sure, she was full, actually fuller than she normally was when she left Bootlegger, but she couldn't have let him win.

Everyone at the table oohed and aahed as Katie put her arms up in the air for a moment before dropping them in her lap and leaning back. She groaned and rubbed her stomach, then looked at Damian with a smile on her face.

Damian laughed. He'd known that she was going to win, but he also knew just how far she would go to get there. She couldn't tell if he had thought it was a good idea just to punish her, or if he wanted to see Eric miserable as well. Either way it was funny, and everyone was laughing and smiling for the first time since the earlier call.

That was worth every single bite of steak to her.

"God." Eric groaned, leaning his head back. "I am going to have to take a chihuahua-shaped ten-pound shit in the morning to relieve this one."

"Oh, my God." Katie winced. "That is so gross. Come on, I just ate that steak. The last thing I want to do is picture you shitting."

"Yeah, that isn't pleasant." Derek laughed. "Not pleasant at all."

"At least I can relax tomorrow and not move," Eric replied.

"And we can watch our show," Katie added.

"What show?" Damian asked.

"Oh, God," Derek said, rolling his eyes. "You had to ask, didn't you?"

"What?" Damian looked around, waiting for an answer.

"It's our soap. There is riveting story lines, love, romance, action, and murder," Katie told him enthusiastically.

Damian laughed. "Why do I doubt that?"

"It's pretty good," Eric admitted. "It's a thing for me, and it was a thing when my crew was overseas. It kind of helped us."

"Really?" Damian said, shaking his head. "Derek?"

"Hey, don't look at me! I don't have anything to do with this." He laughed.

Katie and Eric started talking about the show, filling Damian and Derek in on all the little backstories and what the main characters were facing. By the time they were ready to go they were all engrossed in it, and Katie found that amusing. She hoped that next time the show came on the base audience would be bigger, but probably not. It had still been worth the discussion.

When the tab came Damian grabbed it, paying for everyone's dinner.

Damian smiled. "It's the least I can do for the three of you giving me so much entertainment tonight. Especially you two, with that monster ingestion of cow flesh. You definitely made the steak companies happy tonight."

"My arteries are screaming," Derek remarked. "And I didn't even come close to these two. I have to say though, Katie, for having just eaten half a cow, you look very calm and relaxed—like it was no big thing."

"She is a pro at this," Damian told him. "I had a feeling she was going to blow you two out of the water."

"She only won by one bite," Eric pointed out.

"Out of choice." Katie laughed. "I'm already eyeing my French fries."

"How do you do that?" Eric said, shaking his head. "You are so thin, but you eat like a giant."

"It's one of my special powers." Katie laughed as the waitress brought back Damian's change.

"No, it's yours," he said, smiling at her. "For having to deal with these buffoons."

The waitress looked at the hundred-dollar bill in the check folder and her eyes went wide. She thanked everyone and scampered off to the kitchen, not wanting him to change his mind. That made Katie smile, and just showed again how generous and kind Damian could be.

Derek started working his way out of the booth. "All right, gang, let's get out of here."

Everyone waddled back to the SUV and Katie laughed as she helped push Eric into the car. "Get your fat ass in there!" she huffed.

She rolled in after him and buckled her seat belt, smiling, and relaxed. Damian drove out of the parking lot and headed back toward the base.

Oh! Oh! Pandora yelled.

What? Katie asked in alarm, sitting up straight.

Donutttttsssss, Pandora said, turning Katie's attention to the donut shop coming up in three blocks.

Katie ignored her demon. She didn't even want to entertain the idea, but she was struggling with how loud

Pandora was getting. Pandora was relentless about shit like that.

Pandora chanted, *DoNUTS, doNUTS, doNUTS!*

"No," Katie finally said out loud. "There is no fucking way I am eating another bite. No way in hell."

Damian looked in the rear-view mirror while the other two looked at Katie oddly. Katie groaned, shaking her head and rubbing her hand over her face. She felt like a crazy person sometimes, with Pandora the Ravenous in her head.

"My demon wants donuts," Katie explained. "Sorry."

Eric looked out the window at the donut shop and then at Damian. Damian did a double-take and glanced at Katie in the rearview mirror. Immediately he started to shake his head.

"No," he said pointedly. "I'm not allowing gluttony—or more gluttony—this evening. ERIC! KATIE!"

Everybody burst into laughter as Damian continued shaking his head. He put the pedal to the metal and the SUV's engine revved as they peeled around the turn, getting on the I-15 southbound and hauling ass.

Driving quickly toward the base.

16

By the next morning Katie felt as good as new, an improvement on how she usually felt the day after gorging on food.

Eric had figured he would get to recover the next day, but Korbin had other ideas when he woke everyone up at six in the morning for training.

Katie laughed silently as she got dressed and pulled her hair back in a ponytail.

She knew that Eric would be struggling to even walk that morning, but a workout would do him good. He always was livelier after working out, and he needed to train so that things like the day before didn't happen to him often.

It only took so many times of being cornered by a demon before you weren't lucky enough to find your knife at your side. She enjoyed having fun with the guys, but not at the expense of their mission.

Either way, she was ready to get some training in. She had stiff muscles from the battle the day before.

That wasn't something she normally felt, though to be fair she rarely jumped on countertops, spun in circles, or raced demons, so a little stiffness was to be expected.

She just hoped that getting back into training would help her improve her skills and become better at utilizing the boosts Pandora had been giving her.

She wanted to be faster, tougher, smarter, and deadlier than the demons, and especially ones like T'Chezz. She hadn't forgotten about him.

She knew he was out there somewhere plotting and planning his next move, but she wasn't just going to sit by idly and wait for him to attack. She was going to prepare.

When she was dressed and ready she headed out to the main area, grabbed a muffin, ate it really fast, and went down to start the day. When she walked through the door, she laughed loudly. Eric was dragging himself through the arena, holding his stomach. He looked at her and groaned, his eyes slightly glazed.

She laughed. "Good thing we didn't get donuts!"

"God, I don't even want to think about it," Eric moaned. "I'm gonna go work on weapons and try not to puke."

"Good luck, buddy." Katie shook her head and patted him on the shoulder.

Katie looked around the room, trying to decide where she wanted to start. She had been running through quarterstaff moves in her head for days to get better at it.

She was the kind of girl who didn't give up when she struggled with something. In fact, she was the kind of girl who would just push harder to accomplish her goals.

So long as she didn't have to get up too early. Or at least, earlier. This version of her walked over and grabbed the pole she had made from the dowel and carried it out to an empty area in the arena.

She closed her eyes and breathed heavily in and out, balancing herself, clearing her mind, and getting ready to repeat her practices over and over.

When she opened her eyes she bent her knees, thrusting her right leg out to stabilize her body. She had learned the first time that if she wasn't stable it didn't matter what moves she learned; she would end up on the floor in two seconds flat. She held the stick in both hands and went through a sequence of movements, swiping it through the air with care and patience. As she turned to complete the sequence, her foot twisted and she stumbled to one knee. She growled, angry that she was struggling so hard with the moves.

Relax, Pandora said. *This art is all in your head. You have to visualize each movement before you move into it. You have to see the power and strength it takes. These moves are just the basics, but they will give you the ability to fight someone else and deflect their actions. You cannot move on until you can complete this sequence over and over without thinking about what comes next.*

Katie nodded and stood back up, starting from scratch. She repeated the motions over and over, closing her eyes and letting her body move through them. She could feel the connection with the staff growing stronger as she pivoted, dipped, and swiped it through the air. When she had finished her third walkthrough of the motions, she stood up straight and bowed before opening her eyes.

Wow! Katie exclaimed. *You were right, it is all in my head. How did you know all that? I mean, you don't really seem like the kind of demon who just hung around learning ancient fighting techniques.*

Not everyone I possessed was a business student. She laughed. *Hell, I was lucky to get someone who could read. Usually the smart ones weren't too keen on a ride-along unless it meant they were attempting to take over the world. But for stuff like that, long ago I walked freely among you humans, and I met a man who was proficient in the art. It wasn't ancient then, of course, but I watched and learned almost every day for nearly thirty years.*

Wow, you met a man and stayed with him for thirty years? Katie asked, impressed.

She laughed. *I'm not always about booty.*

What happened to him? Katie asked.

He went off to war and never returned, she told Katie.

Katie could detect a hint of sadness in her voice, and wondered if the big bad demon inside of her had actually loved someone—a human, no less. She wanted to ask, but she knew Pandora would just brush it off to protect her ego. Still, the thought of demons loving was a new concept to Katie. She wasn't sure if it were even possible.

I'm sorry, Katie told her.

Meh. She cleared her throat. *It's a hazard of being human, I guess. You guys are so damn fragile.*

Katie nodded. *We are.*

Pandora went on with the lesson. *Okay, now this is what I want you to do.*

She launched into it, talking about how to hold the

staff, the intention of the motions, and where Katie could take the craft once she had the basics down.

The entire time she talked Katie closed her eyes, focusing on Pandora's voice and moving through the motions over and over until they became so fluid she didn't know where her arm ended and the staff began. She wasn't sure how long she stood there practicing, but when she opened her eyes Korbin and Damian were standing across the room watching her move. Korbin was rubbing his chin.

Hopefully they hadn't caught on to what was going on in her head.

Eric pulled himself up from the weight bench and sat there, wiping the sweat off his brow. Katie walked over and put up her staff, then smiled at him.

He shook his head and stretched his arms up, looking less pale than earlier. "I feel a little better. Nothing to write home about, but better."

"Good," Katie said brightly. "So let's spar."

"Ugh. All right, but the stomach is off limits unless you want to see that steak again," he warned her

"Ew, bro, gross!" Katie wrinkled her nose. "Please don't puke on me."

He walked onto the mat with his hands in the air. "Hey, I'm just being real. Why is it women want truth...until telling the truth is disgusting?"

The two of them squared off, taking easy shots at each

other. Eric was struggling through it, while Katie was pretty much just trying to get him to move his body a little.

She wanted him to get past the steak-induced sloth and get back on track. You never knew when a call would come in, and if one did at that moment, Eric would be taken out in a heartbeat.

Katie blocked a punch and swung around, pulling his arm behind his back. He groaned, feeling the stretch in his shoulder as she leaned toward his ear.

"Don't be sloppy because you don't feel well," she whispered. "That's just an excuse."

"I disagree." He chuckled. "I think it's valid, although it was self-induced."

"Exactly," Katie agreed, releasing his arm and bouncing back into stance.

"Somehow," he turned fast and caught Katie in the arm, "I feel like the slow movements help me think more."

"And thinking leads to giant claw marks in the face," Katie told him, flipping through the air. "You have to move without thinking. You have to know what to do next before it even becomes a question."

"Oh yeah?" Eric chuckled. "And what is next?"

"This." Katie smirked, dropping down and kicking Eric's legs out from under him.

He fell backward onto the floor, and laid there rubbing his stomach. Katie stood up and walked over to him, putting her foot on his chest. He looked up at her and shook his head.

She smiled. "You will get the hang of it."

She reached down and helped him up, slapping him on the back. The two walked off the mat and watched as

Derek and Jeremy started to spar. They heckled the two on the floor from the sidelines as they rested from their own session. Calvin came up next to Katie and smiled as he watched Jeremy and Derek.

"What are you going to do now?" Calvin asked Katie.

"I'm not sure. I haven't really gotten that far yet."

"Why don't you come to the shooting range and practice," he suggested. "Buff up those pistol skills."

"Sounds like a plan." Katie smiled and reached out to grab Calvin's hand, and received an assist to her feet.

She followed Calvin to the shooting range and grabbed a couple of pistols and some ammo. Between clips they talked about the fight at the house. Katie had completely forgotten to ask Calvin how he had done on his first time back out in the field.

"So how was it for you?" Katie asked.

"It was interesting," Calvin replied. "And not because of anything I did."

Katie chuckled. "What do you mean?"

"I was a little nervous at first, sure," he explained, "but Korbin was the one who was all over the place. First he decided to give me some sniper practice by having me duck behind a bush with the sniper rifle, then he became the bait by running along the house and pulling the demons out for me to kill. It was reckless, really—two demons almost took him out. Had I hesitated at all, I would have either missed and the demon would have killed him, or I would have missed and shot Korbin."

"I think he was worried you weren't completely well yet," Katie said. "I mean, I won't lie—I had the same thought. I was worried that you were rushing things with your body. I know *I* was tight and sore, so I can only imagine how you felt."

"Yeah, when I got out there I was definitely thankful that I didn't have to do more than what I did," he admitted. "I guess I was afraid to be weak. Thought that if I was weak, then I would never be strong again. It sounds stupid."

"No," Katie shot back, shaking her head. "It sounds human...something that none of us seem to remember. We *are* human."

"You are right, my dear." He handed Katie another rifle. "Try this one, and then I want you to give the sniper rifle a couple of goes."

"All right," Katie agreed, taking the gun.

"This is the Avtomat Kalashnikova," Calvin explained. "More commonly known as the AK-47. This uses a heavier 7.62-millimeter bullet, and fires a little slower than the comparable American M16 automatic, but is one of the most reliable rifles in the world. It is iconic for the Taliban, but the United States also uses these, or used them heavily in the Iraq war. It's powerful, but reliable."

"Okay," Katie replied, slightly nervous.

She shot at the target and could feel the sheer power behind it, almost losing her balance. The paper was demolished, pieces flying all over the place as if it had exploded. When she was done, she slowly lowered it and handed it to Calvin.

"Wow, that was intense!" She chuckled. "I'm not sure I would ever be comfortable with that thing."

"We use it in situations where we need to do maximum damage very quickly." He took the gun and put it on the cleaning rack. "Now, here is the sniper rifle, but you'll need to move down to the carpeted booth."

Katie moved down to the indicated booth and Calvin brought over the gun. She laid down on the ground to give her stability. She wanted to learn how to shoot it before she went all commando, like Calvin the day before.

"So, the scope… You barely have to put your face up to it," he told her. "You find your target, decide trajectory based on distance, speed, and wind, let out a deep breath, and fire. In here, you should be able to shoot directly at the target."

Calvin pushed the target all the way down the range until Katie couldn't even make out the head on the picture. She cracked her neck and pulled the rifle up to her shoulder. When she leaned forward and looked into the scope, she could see the target straight ahead.

She imagined herself perched somewhere waiting to take out T'Chezz, ready to end it all. Slowly she let out a deep breath and pulled the trigger, letting a single bullet fly. She stood up and took off her goggles as she watched Calvin pull the paper target back.

"Not bad." He laughed as he stared at the hole in the forehead of the target's human figure. "Not bad at all. Now all you need is some of those special bullets, and you will be a demon-killing machine."

"Oh, yeah, I completely forgot!" She turned to Calvin. "I need to visit that bullet-maker here in Las Vegas. He is the one who can help push this to reality."

"Do you think he will be safe enough to work on this project?" Calvin asked.

"I'm not going to have him work on the project," Katie

said, bending down and grabbing the rifle. "I am going to get as much information from him on how to do it as I can. That way Joshua will know, and can start formulating his plan. These bullets are imperative to our cause. Can you imagine if I could just sit on the top of a building with a sniper rifle and pick off demons? I would be out of harm's way, they would die almost instantly, and when we faced the larger beasts we could inflict way more pain. Pain takes away from their concentration, which gives us time to swoop in and be that much more aggressive in taking them out. The pain that metal inflicts could be the difference between life or death for us, or for the innocent."

"Oh, you don't have to sell it to me." He laughed. "You should definitely go take care of that, but I would check out with Korbin first."

"All right," she said, handing him the rifle. "Thanks, Calvin."

"Don't thank me. I still owe you for saving my life."

"No, that's just what we do," Katie replied. "I'm sure in the future there will be more than enough instances where you save mine. Besides, what kind of team would we be without the famed Calvin?"

"That, my dear, is the question," he replied jokingly. "What would the world be like without the famed Calvin in it? It would continue to go on, sure, but would it be a place worth living in? I don't know about that. It would be a lot darker and a whole lot sadder, that is for damn sure."

"You are irreplaceable! Okay, I'll catch up with you later and let you know what I find out."

"Sounds good," he answered. "Be careful."

Katie smiled. "Always."

As Katie walked over to Joshua's workshop, she wondered what research he had done on the rounds for their weapons. She had spoken with Calvin a little on their way back from California after the demon battle in the Inglewood cemetery, and if her memories weren't completely fucked up due to her having been tired, her original idea of just painting the shells with the special metal wasn't the fix they were looking for.

She went past the outer gate and let herself in. There was a lot of movement in the place, and the various machines were making a ton of noise.

Can't we go somewhere else to do this? Pandora asked. *I can't hear you think in here.*

Perhaps I prefer it that way?

It's the internet age, honey. None of your personal thoughts are secret anymore. Whatever you put up on the web five years ago when you were young and drunk is going to bite you on the ass.

Why would anyone be looking for that? I'm dead, remember? Katie motioned to Joshua to get his attention, and pointed to the steps to go down to the basement. Pandora was right, it would be a little less annoying to speak down there.

Who says they are going to look for it? Pandora retorted. *When I put it out there for them to trip over and bust their nose, they will find it quite easily.*

Katie started walking down the stairs. *Ha ha... You can't operate the internet without my arms, and I'm pretty sure I would realize I was typing a command to upload or find something about myself. Plus, I was boring, so there are no horrible pictures of me out there.*

Hell, who needs them to be real? I've heard about Photoshop. Your head, some slut's gorgeous body with a few more curves than you... Ok, a lot more curves than you, and BAM! Instant celeb-slut. Guys will be downloading you like crazy.

Katie walked into the middle of the large room and grabbed a chair near a small table, waiting for Joshua to join her.

She heard Joshua coming down the steps. *Once again, I think I would know it if you were doing something like that.*

"Hi, Katie." Joshua nodded. "How are y-y-you doing?" He grabbed a chair, turned it towards her, and sat down.

Pandora snuck one last comment in. *Not if you were asleep, you wouldn't.*

Bitch! Can you do that? Katie growled. *Dammit! Answer... Fine, don't answer me. NO DONUTS!*

Pandora stayed annoyingly silent.

Katie ignored her mental roommate. "I'm good. I'd like

to hear what you found out about using the metal for bullets?

Joshua scratched his neck for a moment, collecting his thoughts. "Well, I went to one of the best gun shops in the area. It's in Henderson." He put up a hand. "Don't worry, I didn't tell John anything important."

"'John?'" she questioned. "You had to tell him something, right?"

"Well, yes," he agreed. "However, I told him it was for a research project. Somehow he got the impression I was an author." Joshua shrugged. "I should have told him I was a blacksmith. I think he might have been more impressed up front."

I thought you humans adored authors? You used to, Pandora interjected.

That's only if you are Stephen King or George R. R. Martin, Katie replied. *Not so much with other authors. Well, J.K. Rowling.*

I saw something where someone wanted to murder that Martin guy. They were talking about how he was taking too long with his latest book. She sniffed. *I've heard of John Grisham. That Rowling bitch can suck my titties! She didn't have any good PR for demons in her books. What a waste of a great opportunity.*

Does J.K. Rowling even know about you guys? And can you hush for a moment? If you can't hush, then answer my question about doing stuff with my body when I'm sleeping.

Well, that shut Pandora up. At least that concern was semi-useful to her.

"John Kern," Joshua answered, missing Katie's moment of lost focus. "He's the proprietor of Spurlock's in Henderson. They've been open about forty years, and they are on this small stretch of a street that reminds me of an old Main Street."

"And he told you...what? Did he get nosy?"

"Well, I had to wait first. He had a young girl and her mother in there talking about her first rifle. Very customer-focused."

Katie leaned back in her chair, trying to take any stress off him. "If you need to, you can buy some guns and ammo so we aren't just wasting his time."

Joshua just nodded his understanding.

"So, are we going to be able to spray our metal on a bullet?"

Joshua shook his head. "No, that idea won't work. What John talked about was using hollow-points."

"Thought those were banned by the Geneva Convention," Katie interrupted.

Joshua looked at her like she had grown a second head. Katie caught up. "Sorry, my bad.

The demons didn't sign anything like that."

"Technically the US didn't either, at least regarding hollow-points, but they did agree to the spirit of something like that in the past. They've expressed that they might start using them again this year."

Katie waved a hand. "Doesn't matter. Pretty sure we aren't in a legitimate war where the Geneva convention is in place."

Joshua continued, "And cops use them, too. One of the main reasons is so the bullets have a much smaller chance of hurting others by over-penetrating, even if they hit the intended target."

Katie could tell Joshua had been studying the hell out of this. Some of it she knew from her conversation with Calvin, so she wasn't completely clueless.

"Further, if the bullet stops inside the body, there is an argument about hydro-shock causing additional damage. Some scientists argue against it, but the concept has been around since E. Harvey Newton at Princeton wrote a research paper, and the effect was also noted by Colonel Frank Chamberlin during World War II."

Katie could already feel a slight headache coming on and put up a hand. "I'm sorry, give me links to the background information. What did your talk with John... 'Kurns' or 'Kerns?'"

"'E', so 'Kerns,'" Joshua replied. "I think we have a shot if we use a variable hollow-point like a Winchester Black Talon, which today is called a 'Supreme Elite Bonded PDX1.'"

"Why?"

Joshua stuck his right leg out and started searching his pocket for something, pulling out a small piece of metal and handing it to Katie. "That is an example of a reverse tapered jacket. These are specially cut at the hollow to weaken it. When they hit, the six petals open like a flower and the metal inside—which can be our metal—will push into the body."

Katie knew what regular hollow points were like when they hit, but this was almost pretty in its lethality. She looked up at him. "What caliber? .357?"

"Well, it's metric, so 9mm," he told her. "I don't see us being able to make a lot of different varieties, so I'm thinking we go with 9mm so we can ship to all countries if we want. Since the cause of most deaths is bleed-out, we want to put a lot of shots into the victim. You guys' stress level when you shoot is one of the main predictors for getting shots on target, but I'm thinking that a limited recoil could help with faster, more accurate follow-up shots. I also want to give you a higher magazine capacity—"

She finished up the obvious benefit. "Minimizing chances of needing to perform an emergency reload."

He nodded. "The other would be BBs."

Katie blinked a couple of times. "BBs? Like a Daisy BB gun?"

"Sort of," Joshua answered. "I'm calling them BBs, but I'm thinking we would use them in shotgun shells."

"Ohhh," Katie considered the option. Being able to plant fifteen or twenty small balls into the skin of a demon would be damned helpful. "How do you make round balls? Do we have to create molds?"

Joshua shook his head. "Can't do that, too time consuming and problematic. I did as much research as I could, but imagine you have a chunk of clay in your hands. You would roll your hands together until you made the clay a sphere. I understand that is similar, but they have these huge spools of wire. For us to do this, we would have to make spools of wire, then cut the wire to the size we want and manufacture these special disks of steel that will roll the little pieces of wire into balls."

"What a pain in the ass!" She blew out a breath. "So, new machines?"

He shook his head. "No idea," he continued when her expression grew curious. "They don't have pictures of their machine due to proprietary knowledge or something, so I have to design my ideas first and then we get them machined and do tests."

Katie chewed the inside of her lips for a moment. "Let me get Derek and Korbin involved. I bet we can find something on the internet that you haven't, or perhaps get someone involved on the government side. They have to be good for something."

Joshua just kept quiet.

She smiled, slapping her hands on her legs, "So... We have the ideas, we have the path, we need machines, money, skills..." She thought for a moment. "More people, more money... Well, damn."

She tapped a finger on her lips. "If it was easy, everyone would do it." She stood up. "Thanks, Josh. I know we've been hitting you hard for the knives and swords, but I need you to think about how to do this wire, too."

"Ahhh." His eyes lost their focus. "I'll, uh... I'll do that."

She patted him on the shoulder as she passed him, hoping he remembered to go back upstairs when he came back to himself.

Katie tried one more time to get Pandora to answer the question about being able to use her body while she was asleep, but even the threat of withholding donuts didn't budge her. She wasn't sure if Pandora was just being demon-y or truly giving up a secret, so she needed to figure out a way to make sure she wouldn't go on a killing spree when sleeping.

Oh, for fuck's sake! Pandora growled. *You give me donuts, I won't take your sleeping body out for a serial-killing fest.*

Deal...

Weekly! Pandora added.

You can't negotiate after I agree! Katie argued as she waved to the ladies in the shop and let herself out.

I never said how long my agreement was for. It's for a week, and you should have clarified. Be thankful I didn't say an hour! Fuck me, she spat. *I* should *have said an hour!*

One donut per week, Katie agreed.

I never said how many donuts! Pandora huffed when Katie stipulated that.

You should have clarified. Be thankful I didn't say one donut hole.

18

T'Chezz sat back in his chair and stared out the window. He was lost in his thoughts, and oblivious to the world around him. His plan seemed to be failing at every turn, which was more than enraging.

The last kill plan had hit its target, but none of the demons had gotten away.

They'd tried to make it look like the Killers hadn't been there, but they didn't realize that when they killed the demons they came right back down to T'Chezz. He knew his sister had helped the human girl kill six demons on her own, and he knew she was making her stronger for a reason: to kill him. To fight him, and have any chance of surviving.

Knowing that, though, everything now made more sense to him. She was using the girl to protect herself, which was the sister he knew.

She was selfish and self-serving, and didn't really give two shits about anything. The only thing he couldn't understand was why she was allowing the girl to get in the way of the main plan.

T'Chezz looked down at the table in front of him, wondering when the politician would be back. T'Chezz had gotten confidential information from an informant on Earth.

He had said it was information on one of the teams, information that T'Chezz would definitely want to have. He had been searching for the teams, but more importantly for the weapons they were creating.

He needed those weapons, and he needed whoever was behind making them. He couldn't allow them to get in the way of his plans.

He hated that he had been diverted. He was having to think about something other than his plan, but finding the weapons and their maker was necessary in order to keep his demons topside. None of them were surviving very long, and it was all because of that special metal.

T'Chezz was tired of the failures and wanted to take things into his own hands, but he knew it wasn't yet the right time.

Going to Earth at that point could have created a huge problem, and could have easily turned into the end of his plans for at least a couple of centuries. He was tired of sitting around and waiting for things to happen.

So he sent the politician to meet with the informant and bring back the information. T'Chezz wasn't exactly fond of the informant's work recently, but he knew that the man was pretty much the only choice he had at this point. He needed the information and fast, before the Killers took out the rest of his army.

So, after he had summoned the politician and sent him on his way again, T'Chezz sat back and waited for the signal that he was to return.

He had never been very patient, even though one would think that after so many centuries he would deal with waiting a little better. Instead, though, he was struggling to refrain from getting even angrier than he was now.

There was nothing stopping the politician from running off, but T'Chezz knew that his fear was greater than his bravery—and that fear would get T'Chezz everything he would need.

Just as the irritation began to swell again, he got the message from the politician that he was ready to return. T'Chezz closed his eyes and whispered an enchantment in Latin.

"*Huius addis daemonium in inferno, ab inferno ex solo in mea potestate.*"

When T'Chezz opened his eyes the politician was standing nervously in front of him, his human form a little strained from the trip. T'Chezz threw him a piece of cloth to wipe the blood from his nose and stood up, walking over to the window. The man cleaned himself up and caught his breath, and turned toward the demon lord.

"That is always hard on me, coming through the realms," the politician admitted.

"What have you found out?" T'Chezz asked impatiently. "Was the trip worth our time?"

"Yes," the politician told him. "The informant located the Killers, including your sister. They are in a compound near Las Vegas. The base itself is out in the open, but there is nothing around it for miles, just empty desert. You can see the Strip from the base, but finding the base from the Strip is nearly impossible; it blends right into the desert. That is where they live and train, and most likely where you will find these weapons."

"Yes," he said, stroking his chin. "If I know my sister, she will not want to be too far from those weapons—if for no other reason than to save her own damn skin. She doesn't like surprises, so she has always kept her enemies closer than anyone else."

"That is the saying on Earth," the politician said.

"What?" T'Chezz asked, turning toward him.

"Keep your friends close, but your enemies closer," the politician replied.

"I like that." T'Chezz smiled. "Sometimes you humans are smarter than I originally imagined. But you then do stupid things like kill each other over the colors of your skins, and I realize you are an ignorant and barbaric culture that is destined to make the same mistakes over and over."

"That we are," the politician agreed.

"Now, my question is, are you sure this information is true?" he asked. "We all know you didn't do such an admirable job last time."

"I did the best I could under the circumstances," the politician said with irritation. "It's harder up there than you think to not get caught. I have had to sacrifice every-thing to fulfill your wishes."

"Sacrifice?" T'Chezz growled loudly, stepping toward the politician. "I am the one who must sacrifice! I'm stuck down here in this hell, constantly staring at the same walls and the same demons with nothing to do but oversee. I want to *play* again. To broaden my reach. I have waited all this time *patiently*."

"You are right," the politician agreed, bowing his head and backing up on shaking legs. "My apologies."

T'Chezz took a deep breath and turned back to the window. "So?"

"So? Oh, the information," the politician answered nervously. "Yes, I believe the information to be completely accurate."

"And how did you come to this conclusion?"

"Well, I drove past the base—not knowing what it was, but seeing it in the distance—when I went to Las Vegas," the politician explained. "It is right where the informant said it would be, with all of the same attributes: color, etc."

"So you've seen it with your own eyes." T'Chezz rubbed his chin. "Goooood. very good."

"Is there anything else, my lord?" the politician asked.

"Yes," T'Chezz replied. "Go back, stay calm, and act as if nothing is different. Surely if we have found them, they can find us. Start quietly rousing the troops. Let them know something big is coming, and give them my order to be ready for *anything*."

"I will," the politician assured him, bowing.

T'Chezz grumbled, "That was the last time these Killers will get one over on me."

"How did she do the other day?" Korbin asked.

"She did well," Damian admitted. "Though I wasn't with her the whole time, I saw about six piles of dust on the ground floor, most of them in the kitchen or nearby. I am pretty sure she took the brunt of it on her own."

"What about this new training she has been doing?" Korbin asked. "I'm not sure where she is getting the details, but she is getting really good with that staff."

Damian smiled. "She is, and I can't tell you where she is learning it either—but I'm not going to complain."

"Things are definitely changing," Korbin mused. "I just hope we have not unleashed a monster that we can't control."

"Katie isn't a monster." Damian looked at Korbin with granite eyes.

"No, but the demon inside her is." He sighed. "Anyway, so the reporter gave us some news on the politician. Apparently he is going to be at this fancy elite VIP fundraising party in the city."

"*Our* city?" Damian asked.

"Yes, here in Vegas," Korbin affirmed. "It's being held at one of the casinos near Center City. They have several ballrooms and several VIP areas, so they can accommodate a party like this while still staying open to the public. The thing is supposed to be black tie and very elite, and the politician will be there."

"Is he planning something at this event?" Damian asked.

"We don't know," Korbin admitted. "I searched the intel database for the organization but came back with no hits, so we are going off the information from Charlotte. She tracked him down and watched him meet with some demons in suits, and picked up the invite off the table when they had left."

"Are we sending her in?" Damian asked.

"No, I don't think that would be a good idea," Korbin replied. "She is brash, and her face is known to many people in the underground. I don't think she could pull off something like this. They need to be sure she is rich and famous; that she belongs with the VIP's. Charlotte—even dressed up—is a little out there, and I can see it backfiring on her. I don't want to put her in any more danger than I already have."

"What about Katie?" Damian asked. "No one knows her face, she is young, beautiful, cleans up nicely, and is capable of black ops like this with no problem. She could infiltrate the party easily, and once inside her demon would be able to point out not only the politician, but any other demon in the room."

"Do you think we can trust her not to make a scene?" Korbin asked.

"She can restrain her demon," Damian stated. "Especially if we point out the importance of staying undercover throughout this thing. Of course, if she has to engage she has to, but she knows that starting a war like that in the middle of a Las Vegas casino could be a complete and total nightmare."

"That is an understatement." Korbin laughed, leaning back in his chair. "We would lose many innocent lives, much less bringing national attention to what is going on. The less the innocents know, the safer they will be. They tend to turn on each other in times of strife; we have seen that pattern repeated throughout history."

"Absolutely," Damian agreed. "Honestly, I think she is the best person for the job. There aren't many other people who have that kind of intel at the tips of their fingers. If she trusts her demon in this, then we should trust her judgment."

"It's not that I don't have faith in *Katie*," Korbin replied. "It's that I don't have faith in her demon. I worry that she has been bamboozled, and sending her into a place like this could be a complete and total trap. We want her to stay safe, but at the same time figure out what is going on."

"And you are concerned that her demon might give her away," Damian said. "It is definitely a risk, I won't lie."

"But is it an *unnecessary* risk?" Korbin asked.

"Personally, I believe the risk is smaller than you think," Damian said. "This demon seems to want to stay here on this plane. Surely something that powerful knows that if Katie dies, she goes back to hell. I think that the demon will do anything it needs to do to keep her safe. I stand by the idea that if Katie trusts it, I trust Katie's judgment. She has saved multiple lives since she got here, including mine and those of other members of this team. I think I owe it to her to have confidence in her choices. Ultimately, though, it *is* a risk, and in the end it is your call. I will stand by whatever choice you make."

"This mission is close. So close that if we needed to, we could get there very quickly." Korbin spoke aloud, more to himself than Damian.

"And we have the cooperation of the Feds," Damian said. "They could stand by in case they were needed."

"They could," Korbin said, rising and walking over to the window.

He looked down into the training area, thinking about the other day when Katie was completely entranced for hours, moving through the motions with her staff. She didn't waiver; just stayed the course, learning a new skill, trying to fight harder, faster, and more expertly than anyone else.

She truly wanted to be able to face anything that came her way.

She had been like that when she first got there, but at this point she had become a power house—a vital part of their team. Korbin couldn't ignore that fact.

Being the leader was exhausting, trying to juggle what was best for the innocent with what was best for his team. In the end he would always pick the innocent, which was why they were there in the first place.

Still, he couldn't help but worry about sending Katie into a situation that could get her killed without warning. If she found herself in a room filled with demons and her own demon betrayed her she would stand no chance, and there was no way that they could get there quickly enough to help her.

He would be sending the girl into the snake pit, not to mention forcing himself to have faith in a demon. It wasn't what he wanted for her, or for anyone else. Korbin turned back to Damian and sighed, shaking his head.

Damian smiled. "It's like being a father to your team but the caretaker of the world. You have to take care of the world, but you struggle to allow your children to run head-first into a burning building."

"Yes," Korbin agreed. "But unfortunately I can't just sit by idly. I have to make a choice. We will send her in, and hope to God nothing terrible happens."

19

K atie was sitting at the kitchen table, scanning through the different sections of the paper, looking for anything that seemed out of the ordinary. She did that every day, tracking strange killings, possible demon sightings, and interesting news about the rich and famous, who seemed to get richer by the day.

It was her own little reconnaissance. Something to keep her busy connecting different dots, and ultimately she hoped it would help clarify the bigger picture in some way, shape, or form.

She knew Derek had the website and Korbin had tons of informants as well as getting information from the higher-ups, but she couldn't just stand by like a weapon they pointed in the correct direction at need, then patted her on the back when it was over.

She was more than that, and she wanted to make sure that when the time came Korbin saw that.

She could find things. She could do detective work; she

showed that when she'd helped Calvin track Charlotte down. She wanted that to continue, so he would give her assignments beyond incursions.

She understood Korbin had reservations about her, and that he was nervous taking a chance on her demon in an uncontrolled situation. She wanted to make him feel comfortable in the fact that she had everything on track and under control.

Without missions other than ass-kickings, though, she was never going to convince him that her demon was not going to cause a huge problem—at least not with the other demons.

I don't know why you care, Pandora wondered.

Ugh, get out of my thoughts, Katie grumped.

The fact that you could beat the pants off any demon or man should be enough for him to let it go, Pandora told her.

It would be just like you to say I should rule by fear, Katie chided. *I don't want my team to be afraid of me. I want them to trust me a hundred percent.*

And most of them do, Pandora replied. *So what is so important about Korbin?*

He's the leader of this group and the one who has to make the hard decisions, and I don't want him to ever have to make that decision when it comes to me, Katie explained, looking down at her buzzing phone. *He's calling right now.*

Pandora sighed. *All right, answer away.*

She put the phone to her ear. "Yes, boss?"

"Hey, are you busy?" Korbin asked.

"Nope," Katie said, closing the paper.

"Will you come to my office? I have something to ask of you," Korbin said.

"Sure, be right down," she replied, pressing End.

Katie tidied her notes and headed downstairs, curious what Korbin wanted to talk to her about.

She hadn't made any waves recently. No random clawed hands, no crazy moves in training, no new cars, and there hadn't been any incursions that she knew of.

Part of it made her nervous, like one day she would go down there and he would tell her that she was being transferred to research—or that he had to make the hard decision.

She didn't want to become another statistic, so she had to keep her cool and keep Pandora locked down and on the same page with her.

"Hey there!" Korbin stood as she walked in. "Please take a seat."

"Okay." Katie smiled. "What can I do for you?"

"We got that intel from Charlotte we were looking for," he started. "We know where the politician will be tonight."

"That's great." Katie nodded, blowing out her breath. "Should we put a team together to snag him?"

"Actually, no. We know where he is going to be, and we don't want to make this any more public than it has already become. We would like you to go in undercover and find out if the politician is a real problem or just someone in our way. There is a possibility that he is just a diversion, put there to lead us down the wrong path. We can't take any chances, though, not when it comes to so many people. He will be attending a VIP party tonight, and we want you to go in like you belong and get the information from him discreetly but quickly. We don't want to find out the hard way that there is something perched outside, just waiting to come in and do some real damage."

"Right," Katie agreed. "And what information are you looking for?"

"When the next attack will be, who is behind all this, and where he stands in the order of things," Korbin listed.

"Do you want me to kill him?"

"No." Korbin shook his head. "Leave him unharmed when you are done. We want to follow him; see where he ends up."

Where he will end up, they can't follow, Pandora remarked.

"All right, I'll do it," Katie told him.

"Good." He smiled. "I'll send the invite information to your email. And please be careful! We don't know how many demons will be at this thing, hiding behind their humans."

"Always careful," Katie assured him, standing up. "It's my middle name."

"Right." He chuckled.

Pandora sniffed. *"Katie 'Careful' Maddison" has a horrible ring to it.*

Katie left the office and headed back upstairs, excited about the opportunity. It was exactly what she had wanted; exactly what she had been hoping he would allow her to do.

She had finally gotten an undercover gig she was pretty sure she was going to kick ass at, but when she got to her room and pulled up the invitation her heart sank just a bit. The party was super-elite and super-fancy, and she was going to have to do some serious work to fit in with those people.

She had grown up poor. She had never been to an event like that in her life. The most expensive party she ever had gone to was her senior prom, and even then she had worn a hand-me-down dress and her mother's shoes.

Don't worry, Pandora told her. *I got this. If you want to glam yourself up, you have come to the right place. I have been around during every pertinent fashion wave in history. I know timeless and classic like the back of my hand...and I know slutty and hot as well. Fortunately for you, you will need to be a very good mixture of both. You have a hot body and rocking cheek-bones, and I have been working on the rest. I know exactly how to get us into this thing.*

Why does that make me incredibly nervous? Katie wondered.

Because you know I will make you fabulous, and you are happy in your drab clothes, frumpy panties, and makeup-less face, Pandora replied. *Because you know that I have it in me to make you desirable to the whole world, but you would rather sit around moping about killing demons.*

You are a bitch, you know that?

I know, Pandora exclaimed happily. *It's one of my best attributes, actually. Well, that, and my seduction abilities.*

Katie climbed into her car, and put the top down, making sure her hair was securely tied back. She hated shopping even more than she hated gorging herself on food.

She never knew what to buy. She didn't feel comfortable in the trendy clothes, and salespeople always tried to get her to wear low-cut shirts and skimpy skirts that barely covered her ass.

She had never been that kind of girl, even in her non-Damned form. She liked to be comfortable, so if she couldn't wear what she wanted she usually didn't go to whatever event it was.

She also didn't do Halloween, since it had just been an excuse for the girls in her college to be sluts and wear almost nothing. She just chilled, comfortable in her jeans, t-shirts, and recently spandex pants and flack vest.

Okay, tell me where you want me to go, Katie said.

Wherever you shop, Pandora replied.

Target?

Oh, for fuck's sake. Pandora sighed. *Go to the Strip. I saw a Neiman Marcus there, so we can start with that. They carry all the high-fashion designers, so we should be good.*

Okie dokie. Katie turned off the 15 and onto Spring Mountain Road.

And stop saying that. No one with an ounce of class says "okie dokie," Pandora snapped.

Yep, Katie replied with a smirk. *Relax, I know how to talk to people. You just focus on the outward appearance.*

Whatever, Pandora answered.

When they got to Neiman Marcus, Katie got out and handed her keys to the valet.

She was amazed at how differently she was treated when she pulled up in a car like hers.

She resented that, knowing how amazing a woman her mother was and that she didn't get that kind of treatment because she didn't drive a fancy car or go to fancy places.

She pushed the thought out of her head and walked

inside, pretty much letting Pandora take over for this part. She tried on about twenty dresses, and fought Pandora on the final choice.

Eventually, though, she just gave in.

Afterward she purchased some very expensive make-up from their counter after the person spent an hour working on her face, telling her how best to apply their product. She bought some perfume, to boot.

By the time she was done shopping, her wallet was crying, even though she would be reimbursed since it was for a mission, and her arms were aching from carrying all the bags. It was incredibly annoying to have to do all that just so she could get in the door of an elite event.

Katie was pretty sure that if she lived that life all the time, she would go very few places. It was a huge hassle, and they hadn't even gotten home yet.

When they did arrive back at the base, almost everyone was out for the day. Katie was very happy about that. She did not need the guys teasing her about getting all dolled up for this thing. She just wanted to get it over with. Originally she had been excited about it, but after realizing what kind of hell she was going to have to go through just to walk through the doors, she was starting to regret her decision to attempt to make Korbin trust her more.

Shit, she had been doing just fine.

All right, first you should take a shower, Pandora ordered. *When you get out, I am going to take over so I can do your hair and makeup.*

Fine, she grumped. *Can I at least have a chair to sit down on?*

Stop being a baby, Pandora snapped.

Katie showered quickly, shaving her legs and her armpits so that Pandora would stop yelling at her about the stubble.

Pandora argued, *No one with an ounce of pride in themselves—and a Ferrari—will go out with stubble, and neither should you.*

She climbed out and gave her body over to Pandora, just standing there as the demon took care of her body, tweezing her brows and otherwise abusing it.

When that was done, she put on the silk robe she had bought that day and let Pandora blow-dry her hair and then set it in large Velcro curlers.

When Pandora was done with that, Katie grabbed a bottle of water from the mini fridge in her room and took control back for just a minute.

I am shaved, tweezed, and dried. Now what? Katie asked.

Now we make your face a bit more presentable.

Katie pouted. *"Why do you have to make it sound like I am some hideous beast?*

Oh, shut up, Pandora told her. *You know you aren't hurt by my comments.*

You're right. Katie shrugged. *Let's just get this over with.*

Katie grabbed the bag of makeup and walked back into the bathroom, unloading everything and lining it up on the counter.

She had no idea what some of the pieces were for. It was looking more like a medieval torture chamber than a girl's bathroom. Katie took a deep breath and let Pandora take over, standing there watching as she blotted different creams all over her face. When she was done with that and her face had dried, Pandora applied the concealer, sponging it on very carefully.

This stuff is awesome, Pandora said. *Makeup was not this good last time I was here.*

Great, Katie replied. *I'll send a fax to the manufacturer to tell them their makeup has a demon queen from hell's seal of approval.*

You know, you can be a real bitch.

This time it was Katie who kept quiet.

When Pandora was done with the foundation, she ran a brown pencil over Katie's eyebrows and applied dark colors to her lids, just like the smoky-eye look Katie had seen in the magazines a hundred times. Pandora really was quite good at makeup. When it was time for her eyeliner, one eye went perfectly but Pandora accidently jabbed the pencil in her other eye.

Ouch! Katie shrieked. *For fuck's sake!*

Sorry. I am doing someone else's makeup from inside their body. The depth perception is pretty strange.

God, why do I have to wear makeup? Katie complained, wiping at her eye. *You looked good without makeup when I first saw you.*

Yes, I did, Pandora affirmed. *And if you would let me change your body, so would you.*

Kate sat there for a moment, waiting for Pandora to fix the eyeliner and finish up the second eye. When she was done Katie took her body back, exasperating Pandora.

How am I supposed to finish this if you keep taking over? Pandora growled.

What about your gravity-defying breasts? Katie asked.

She laughed. *Is that what would tempt you?*

It's definitely a start, Katie told her. *I mean, you gave me these huge tits, but didn't think about the fact that they have to stay upright. The dress you made me buy—there is no way these puppies are staying in line without a bra, and a bra with that dress is impossible.*

Why didn't you say something about this earlier? Pandora asked. *I could have fixed that issue from the beginning.*

I don't know. Katie shrugged. *Didn't seem necessary.*

Well, first we need to finish your makeup, Pandora replied, snatching control back from her. *Now I am going to curl your eyelashes, and after I do that I will apply mascara.*

With what? Katie asked.

This. Pandora held up an eyelash curler.

Oh, God, Katie moaned.

Just hold on tight, Pandora replied. *This won't hurt a bit...*

2 0

When Katie pulled up in front of the hotel in her blue Ferrari, the valet came running to open the door. Katie pressed her black Jimmy Choo heels to the pavement and stood up, smiling sweetly at the valet.

He took her keys and handed her a tag, which she put into her purse.

As she walked, her sparkling black gown fluttered around her. The straps rose from a very deep V in the front and wrapped around her neck like a choker.

The skirt hit the floor, hugging her curves with a slit the went halfway up her thigh. She pressed her ruby-painted lips together and flipped her loose black curls back over her shoulder.

She was fucking hot; desirable—and completely badass —in her dress.

When she got inside she walked directly back to the VIP section, where she had no problem at all getting in.

The doorman didn't even check a list. He just moved to the side and held the door open for her.

She smirked at him flirtatiously and went inside. There wasn't a single person in the joint who believed she wasn't someone incredibly important. She was starting to *feel* important, and her strut picked up.

Look at you! Pandora marveled. *You look fucking amazing.*

Everyone is being so nice to me, Katie replied. *It feels weird.*

Of course they want to treat you nicely, Pandora assured her. *No one with this body in this dress with these tits is going to be turned down for anything, especially not in a place that desperately wants your money.*

It helped a lot that I showed up in an almost three-hundred-thousand-dollar Ferrari, Katie agreed. *The body is great, sure, and the dress is hot, but no one is going to care unless the outside matches the inside. And let's face it, wearing ten grand worth of clothes and makeup and driving that car definitely boosted their confidence in my importance.*

Yeah, but the body gets you the attention, Pandora replied.

Let me just remind you that we are in Vegas. Katie discretely adjusted her boobs. *Which means that there are a million women in this town with tits like this, although theirs are silicon. But the Ferrari is money, baby.*

Katie carefully walked through the crowd. She was only in the normal VIP area, so she still needed to find the special VIP event area. That was where the politician would most likely be.

She wanted to fit in, though. She didn't want to look like she was searching for something, since that might look suspicious. She walked to the bar and ordered a Cosmo, then stood there sipping it as she looked around the room.

There were a lot of heavy hitters there, and several of them were adorned with red ringed eyes just like she had figured they would be. As she moved her eyes across the back of the room, she saw the special event entrance. Two doorman stood guard, and the richest of the rich walked in and out.

I found them, Katie told Pandora.

Good, she replied. *Now stop looking like James Bond and start looking more like Pussy Galore.*

Katie smiled and looked at a group of guys who were ogling her outfit. She blushed, realizing that between what her cleavage revealed and the slit up her thigh, she was more uncovered than she'd been in most bathing suits she had owned in the past. She drank the rest of her Cosmo and pulled her skirt over her bare leg.

Good lord! I said Pussy Galore, not Little House on the fucking Prairie. Pandora groaned. *Smile at those men, then get your shit and head over to the event area. We need to get inside.*

Katie sighed. *Yes, ma'am.*

She already wanted to leave. She just wanted to go back to base and forget all about her desire to be more useful. This place was a blatant example of everything that was wrong with their world.

A bunch of rich men parading around in expensive suits with wads of cash in their hands, gambling away the money they took from the poor to buy their next gas-guzzling jet. The women were all scantily clad and eager to meet these men, wanting no future beyond finding a rich husband to make them rich.

Katie didn't understand it at all.

Where was the substance? Where were the conversations about important topics? Where was the account-ability for where the money was coming from in the first place? Katie wondered how many of those rich men had become what they were only after a demon took their bodies.

More than you might imagine, Pandora said darkly.

Katie had thought it would be more difficult to get into the event area, but all she had to do was flash the doorman the picture of the invite she had saved on her phone and let him ogle her tits for a second, and she was in.

They wandered around for a while, watching the people gamble, learning about the random charity that no one there actually cared about, and nonchalantly trying to hunt down the politician.

Katie had looked him up online before leaving the base so she would know exactly what he looked like. She figured if there happened to be more than one demon in the crowd, she would need to narrow it down.

It was a good thing she had, because more people in that place were Damned than not.

Katie walked over to one of the random cocktail tables and stood there sipping a glass of champagne a waitress offered her. Her eyes moved from face to face in an attempt to find the mad politician.

Near the back, where the craps table was located, the sea of people parted almost ceremoniously and there was the politician. He was living it up at the craps table, surrounded by adoring fans and one security guard, who was wearing sunglasses.

There he is, Katie said to Pandora. *Why am I not surprised that he is as skeevy as he looked on the internet?*

Even more so, Pandora grumbled. *I can't believe women sleep with men like that. They are so fucking gross.*

I know, Katie agreed. *It astounds me every time I hear on the news that another of our politicians has been caught with his pants around his ankles.*

I'm starting to understand why you have become a man-hater, Pandora said.

Katie chuckled. *I am not a man-hater. I'm a stupid-person-hater, and it just so happens that most of the men I knew before the team were stupid.*

Mmmhmm, Pandora teased.

Katie sighed. *Anyway, I need to figure out how to get this politician alone. I mean, it shouldn't be too hard since he is a man and I have giant tits now. Men are pretty simple creatures.*

You sound more and more like me every day. Pandora sighed. *I love it. Yeah, we need to get you over there and have you start flirting.*

Where is he going?

To that fancy-ass bathroom over there. Trust me, okay?

All right. Katie sighed and let Pandora take over her body.

Pandora strutted Katie's body toward the bathroom. She fluffed her breasts, pressed her lips together, and flipped her hair back over her shoulder. She stopped in front of the security guard and smiled.

"This one is occupied," he told her.

"I know," she replied, reaching up and playing with the

end of his tie. "It just so happens that your boss in there was asking about a hot body to play with earlier. I wanted to come over and accommodate him, because in all reality, baby, there isn't a slut here who is hotter than me, I promise you that. And maybe when he's done, you can come in and give me some more. I bet I know which of the two of you is the bigger man, and I'm not talking about your height, sweetheart."

Pandora was laying it on as thick as she could, wanting to get into that bathroom before he came out. She walked forward again, this time stopping just inches from the big guard's muscular chest.

She stretched up and whispered close to his lips, "You wouldn't want to disappoint your boss, would you? I'm sure he would be more than happy with you if you sent a hot little thing like me in there to take advantage of."

"And who would be taking advantage of whom in that situation?" he asked.

"Well, he would, of course. He wants the power." Katie smiled. "But you... I would climb right up in that lap and ride you till the lights went out in Vegas."

He cleared his throat and smiled, then reached back and grabbing the door handle. Katie looked around the room to make sure no one was watching and slipped inside, closing the door behind her. She stood there with her feet spread wide and put her hands on her hips. The politician shook himself dry and zipped up his pants, then turned to wash his hands. He was obviously surprised to see her standing there.

She looked at him with dark eyes and smirked. "Do you need to run? Or do you have a minute to, well, *talk?*"

He looked Katie up and down and stuck one hand in his pocket, then tilted his head toward her, the red glow in his eyes too visible to not signify a demon. Pandora forced a smile onto Katie's lips, even though she was starting to fight back.

"I think I have a minute for you," he said, strolling past her and cracking open the door.

Katie moved farther into the bathroom and waited.

"Don't allow anyone in here for a few moments," he told his guard, then glanced back at Katie. "Actually, make that twenty minutes."

He closed the door and flipped the lock, straightening his collar before turning toward Katie. He reached down for his belt buckle and began to walk toward her, mumbling under his breath.

"I'm about to rip a new hole in this slut," he whispered, licking his lips.

As soon as he was close enough, Katie reached forward quickly and grabbed him by the throat, lifting him off the floor and then slamming him against the wall. Her eyes glowed red and she held tightly to his throat, making sure he couldn't speak at all. He tried to open his mouth, but she tightened her grip and then punched him square in the gut.

The guard remained outside, nodding at the people who passed. He jumped slightly when the banging sounds started inside of the bathroom.

The guard shifted his stance. He had a slight grin on his face, thinking about the hot, hard sex going on in there. He knew his boss was a bit of freak, especially with the demon in him, but he hadn't known he liked it like that.

To each his own. The guard definitely didn't blame him. She was one hot piece of ass.

He heard another *BANG* as a body or bodies slammed into a wall, and tried to hide a smile. Damn, that man was punching it hard!

Inside the bathroom, though, it was a completely different story.

Katie turned and tossed the politician on the floor, standing over him as he pulled himself to his knees. He put his hands in front of him and whimpered, both his demon and his human self-cowering in their presence. Katie pulled back her arm and started to swing when the politician called out, putting his hand in the air.

"Please," he begged, shaking. "Please don't. I'll make you a deal. I'll give you some information—information you are going to want—in exchange for my life."

"What is the information?" Katie said.

"No, fuck that," Pandora exclaimed through Katie's mouth. "This scumbag doesn't deserve to live. Let me just rip his fucking throat out and eat that motherfucking demon inside him."

"No." Katie sighed. "We came here for a purpose, and I want to hear his information."

The politician watched Katie nervously, listening to her demon and then her human self talking out of the same mouth.

He was blown away by that, unsure how it was even being done. He had a pretty strong demon, but he didn't have the ability to do *that*.

"Look, I know you want this dirt bag." Katie continued arguing with herself. "But let him go for now. We will get our revenge on him later. He is the one who brought the beast to LA, the demon breathing down our damn necks. I want revenge as much as the next person, but we can't miss out on this information," She sneered at the politician. "If it is any good. If not?" She drew a line across her throat.

"And then what?" Pandora argued. "He goes back and tells T'Chezz? That will do us a lot of good. We won't make it out of this place alive."

"That's what we do," Katie snapped angrily.

"Fine," Pandora yelled. "Fine, spare his little pathetic human life."

"Thank you," he whined. "Thank you so much."

"Shut up!" Katie slapped him across the face and he bounced against the wall, then fell back to the floor. "Give me the information before I lose my patience."

"There is a hit out on Korbin's Killers," he told her frantically.

"When?" Katie hissed, getting down in his face.

"Uh… Uh…" He looked down at his watch. "In thirty-two minutes!"

"Fuck," Katie screamed, slamming a foot into the wall and yanking it back out. She grabbed him by the hair. "So help me God, if one person on that base gets even a scratch, I won't just fucking kill you, but I'll let my *demon* kill you. Do you *fucking* understand me?"

"Yes!" he whimpered.

"Just fucking kill him," Pandora insisted.

Katie dropped him. "A promise is a promise."

"Yeah, but you only promised to spare the human," Pandora said evilly.

"You're right," Katie agreed, narrowing her eyes. "And it

will only take thirty seconds to pull that dirty mother-fucker out of him."

"Oooh, pleeeeease!" Pandora begged.

Katie smiled. "I actually think that it's a fantastic idea."

"NO," the politician shrieked, putting up his hands as Katie started to walk toward him.

Her eyes flared red. "If you think that was bad, you ain't seen nothin' yet." She laughed, A monstrous hand reached down and pulled the screaming demon out of the politi-cian's body.

As soon as the demon left his body, the politician fainted.

Katie smiled, holding the demon in the air as Pandora devoured its soul. When the demon was gone and the echoes of his screams had dissipated, Katie straightened her dress and hair and cracked the bathroom door, closing it behind her.

"He might need a few minutes to get his energy back," she told the guard. "He said he wants you in there in no less than ten minutes, no more than eleven. Got that?" She patted him on the chest. "Sorry, maybe another time?"

His look was forlorn as she walked away.

Katie moved fast through the crowd, trying to make it out to her car so she could get back to base and warn them in enough time. Her phone was dead now, dammit, and her earpiece had fallen out of her ear when she was dealing with the politician.

She felt almost frantic, like her family had been threat-ened. She wished she had just slit the man's throat and been done with it, because he'd had no remorse.

Oh, he is a dead man walking, Pandora told her.

What do you mean? Katie asked.

I mean that he has had that demon in him for so long, his body needs its energy like a damn drug. I doubt he will survive three weeks.

Katie smiled as she made her way out of the building and to the valet. *Good.*

Katie slammed her foot down on the gas pedal and hauled ass toward the base. She had to wait until she could slow down to get her phone plugged in, because cops had picked up her tail right after she jumped on the 15. She just went faster, though, leaving them in the dust behind her.

She sped down the 15, weaving between the cars to get to the base as fast as possible.

She looked ahead and saw a semi pulled off to the side of the road. She could hear the sirens getting louder so she veered to the shoulder, sped around the semi, and parked behind it, making herself invisible to everyone passing by. She sat there for a minute until all three cop cars went by, then pulled back out on the highway and u-turned it to head back north toward the Strip.

As soon as the dusty road came up on her left, Katie squealed her tires turning down it. She could see the compound in the distance.

The compound had been a small business park back in the day, but it had gone bust years before and the team had acquired it as their base.

All Katie knew was that her family was in there—the only people she had in the entire world—and they were going to be hit by an ambush, but had absolutely no idea. It had all been a setup from the first moment, but nobody had seen it.

She stopped at the old broken-down sign and shook her head in anger as she reached down and pulled off her heels. She tossed them in the back seat and grabbed the phone out of her purse.

She plugged it in, and as soon as it booted she dialed Korbin's number and hit the speaker button. It rang a couple of times, but finally he picked it up.

"Katie," he exclaimed. "Your comm went out."

"I know," she replied. "I had to get a little rough with the politician."

"Are you all right?" he asked.

"Yes. No, I mean you guys are in deep shit," she told him. "The demons are coming for the team at the compound. They are supposed to hit you in less than ten minutes."

"What? What are you talking about?"

"That politician...he traded his life for the secret," she said. "The secret was that Korbin's Killers were going to be hit in thirty-two minutes, but that was back at the event. You need to batten down the hatches and get loaded for bear. Seriously, something bad—or several somethings—are going to hit us. I would have called earlier but I hadn't set up Bluetooth and I there were police on my ass."

"Where are you?"

"I'm a few minutes away. I can see you. This is serious. Get everyone to safety. As soon as I can I will be there, and I promise I will help handle this problem."

"Just be safe," Korbin told her. "We are going to be okay."

Katie pressed End, threw the phone on the passenger seat, and floored it again. She was on a concrete road that headed from the 15 to the compound. The whole thing was open desert, so she couldn't cut across without getting stuck. She leaned forward, slamming her hand on the steering wheel and pushing the car as fast as it could go while still maintaining control.

It was so damned typical that something like that would happen. Everything had been going so smoothly. She never —not in a million years—expected those words to come out of the politician's mouth.

She shook her head and straightened her back, then noticed something strange half a mile ahead and off the road about a hundred yards. It was waving—shimmering, almost—and she could see demons appearing out of nowhere. She frowned and leaned forward for a better look.

"What the fuck is that?" Katie mused aloud.

That *is a rift in the fabric of reality*, Pandora informed her. *A way for the demons to come and go from hell to Earth and back. It takes a fucking lot of power to open something like that. The last time it happened... Well, let's just say God came crashing down.*

Katie bit back a curse. *I don't have fucking time for the apocalypse. We have to shut it. How do you close it?*

You have to block it, Pandora explained.

That's a big fucking hole, Katie argued. *Unless we throw something big through it, a damned army could come through.*

We don't have *anything big. We are in the middle of the fucking desert. Unless you've got a piano in your pussy?* Pandora wondered.

Why would I have a piano in my vagina? Katie yelled back, looking around for anything she could use.

"*Well, there aren't ever any dicks in it, so who the fuck knows what you store in there?*"

Katie looked around her and realized that Pandora was right—there was nothing. Then she had an idea, albeit one that made her stomach cramp and her head ache.

"*DAMMIT!*" She sighed and shook her head. She couldn't believe her luck. She twisted the wheel and pressed down hard on the gas, sending the car racing across the desert.

She swerved wildly, dodging the cacti and trying to keep the thing going fast enough that they wouldn't get bogged down in the sand.

What are you doing? Pandora yelled.

Katie watched at least thirty snarling demons run from the rift toward the base. Among those thirty were three that seemed just as big as the one in LA, if not larger.

She'd had a hard enough time trying to take down one of those motherfuckers with Calvin. How the hell was she going to tackle a whole army of them? There was nothing normal about the situation, so all Katie could do was grip the steering wheel tightly and drive full steam ahead toward the rift.

She wouldn't let the demons hurt her family.

"Holy shit," Katie, gaping. "Are you fucking kidding me?"

Just when she thought things couldn't get any worse, a fourth seriously huge demon started to appear. The thing's leg alone was as big as the demon in Los Angeles had been, and his aura rippled around him. Katie slammed her foot down on the gas and gunned it straight for him.

Fucking hell, bitch, Pandora screamed. *You can't go in there!*

"I don't plan to," Katie yelled aloud.

"You are a crazy biiiiiitch," Pandora yelled in her brain as Katie was yelling aloud.

Katie aimed the car at the emerging demon and swung open the door, waiting until the last few seconds before throwing herself out of the car. She rolled across the sand, groaning and grunting as the car hit rocks and various desert flora.

She slid to a stop and looked up in time to see the car slam into the demon, both her car and the demon being thrown back through the rift.

The hole blinked out of existence as the massive demon went back to hell, Katie's car going with him. She put her hands on the sand and growled as she watched sparks shoot from the rapidly closing rift.

The biggest demon was gone for now, but there were still a good number of them heading for the base. Katie couldn't believe she had just jumped from her car before sending it plunging into the fiery depths of hell.

She was pretty sure there was nothing in her insurance plan that covered paranormal rifts.

Uh, Pandora? Katie pulled out a couple of cactus spines. *Was that your brother?*

Katie glanced down at her legs to examine the sand-rash that covered them. There was a rip in her very expensive couture dress, but she had to give it to Pandora—her dress was still firmly in place where it counted. Still, jumping from a car in an evening gown was probably not the best idea she'd ever had.

I think that was *the fucker*, Pandora admitted. *He was taller than I remember.*

Katie stood up and spitting out sand, *Well, he owes me a motherfucking car.*

With that she took off toward the base, trying to get there in time to help the others. Without a leader the demons would be slowed down, but not that much. They already had a head-start on her, so she had to pick up the pace.

"And not just any car," Katie yelled in frustration. "That fucker owes me a brand-new Ferrari California T in California Blue with all the fucking bells and whistles."

I'm sure he will be happy to oblige, Pandora snarked.

Okay, I'll just take his head instead," Katie growled, her eyes shining red.

That is something I can definitely get behind, Pandora yelled, boosting Katie's speed. *But first we have to save the others.*

Korbin grabbed his phone and walkie-talkie, then hit the alarm and ran toward the stairs, taking them two at a time all the way to the personal quarters level. He burst through the door to find everyone standing in the living area.

He raced across the room to the stairwell door and slammed it shut, locking it tightly, then turned and let them see the anger boiling on his face.

He pointed at his men. "Eric, Jeremy, Damian, and Derek, I want you to go to all the entrances of this building and lock them down, including the roof hatch. Demons are on their way here. We don't know how many yet, but they will be here any moment. Calvin, come with me. We have to get everyone else to safety."

Korbin and Calvin ran down to the training level and through the secret passage into the workshop.

They didn't even stop to say anything to Josh, who happened to be sticking something into the locked shelving. They just bolted up the stairs to the top floor where all the women were working.

Mamacita stood up from her chair and stared at the men. Something was clearly happening.

Korbin ran to the front doors and slammed them closed, then sealed them, locking everyone in the building. When he looked out the small window at the top of the steel door, he could see the demons running toward the compound. They were much closer than he'd figured they would be.

There were so many. At least thirty, and led by three very large demons. Korbin whipped around to face the girls, who had gathered around him.

He pointed to the stairs. "Everyone get to the basement. This is *NOT* a drill."

Some of the girls whimpered and others shrieked, but

everyone moved with haste, including Mamacita. Korbin stood at the top as Calvin ushered everyone down to the basement. Mamacita was the last to leave the manufacturing floor.

"Is that everyone?" Korbin asked her.

"Yes." She nodded and headed down the steps.

Korbin slammed the large heavy door they had just installed and sealed it shut, then stood there for a moment to collect himself before heading down the stairs. The girls clung to each other with fear on their faces.

"The enemy, which are demons, have found our base and they are attacking," he explained. "You should be safe, but *you have to stay down here, out of the fight.* Understand me?"

"What if they break through?" one of the girls asked.

"Then you grab whatever you can and you fight with everything that you have," Korbin answered. "Joshua's metal will hurt them, and if you cut off their heads they die instantly. Don't be a hero. Help your sisters, help each other, and do the best you can to survive. We are going to keep them away from here the best that *we* can."

Korbin turned to Joshua as the girls went off to Mamacita, looking for comfort. He knew this was a shock to a lot of them, but he knew also that Mamacita would work hard to keep them all in one piece. They were his responsibility, though, and he had to make sure they stayed safe.

"Do you have any new weapons?" he asked Josh.

"Yes, over here," he replied, leading them over to cabinets. "Take whatever you need."

Korbin smiled at Joshua. "Thanks."

They grabbed a few extra knives and a couple of swords before they headed through the tunnel toward the base. Korbin shoved a knife into Joshua's hand and grabbed his shoulder.

He looked him in the eye for a moment, and then at the women.

"Make your family proud, Joshua," he told the young man. "Fight if you have to. Defend your home, your birthright, and the women here, who are part of our team."

"I will," he told Korbin confidently.

Korbin nodded and glanced back at Mamacita one last time.

He pulled the door closed behind him, leaving the others in the enclosed space. Joshua turned the large wheel on his side to completely seal the structure.

They were stuck in that box and they had no idea how long they would be there. It was a chilling feeling even for Joshua, who had seen his fair share of demons through his father.

He knew he could protect them, though, and he would —whatever the cost.

Mamacita eyed Joshua as he stood in front of the doors to the underground tunnel, holding his knife firmly in his hand. He was no longer the scared little boy she had first met.

He looked like an angry man; a warrior, perhaps a shadow of his father.

She understood that he would not just sit there and wait while the others fought, and frankly she wasn't sure she would either.

She went to the weapons closet and opened it, tilting her head at two weapons hanging from the back.

They shimmered and sparkled like the others, but these seemed special.

They were identical sais, with strong carved-ivory handles and tips that looked like they could shatter diamonds.

She reached in and ran her fingers down one of the blades, admiring the craftsmanship that Joshua had put into them. They were beautiful, even more so than some she had seen across the ocean so long ago.

Memories gently floated through her mind and she sighed, remembering her early life. Joshua walked up beside her and nodded as he looked into the closet.

He blushed, realizing she'd found his work, but she didn't know why he would be embarrassed. It was some of the finest she had seen from him, including the swords he had made for the others.

He should be proud of these, but he probably assumed that no one would understand them, especially not on Korbin's team.

They weren't very skilled in karate, or anything of that level. They fought with their muscle instead of their minds, which was okay—just not workable with the sais.

"When I was growing up, I wanted to be a fighter," Joshua explained. "But because of my difficulties, my mother wouldn't let me do it. When I was old enough to watch television, I got hooked on *Teenage Mutant Ninja Turtles*. They were all outcasts; different than everyone else, but inside, where it mattered, they were *warriors*—skilled warriors. They knew what it took to be the best, and though they ate a lot of pizza, they made sure they *were* the best."

"That's a nice story," she told him.

He chuckled. "Yeah. Anyway, I made the sais because they were my favorite weapon on the show, and I hoped that someone else would like them and be able to use them. So far I haven't met anyone who is knowledgeable about using them or even knows anything about karate, so I leave them hanging there, hoping one day they will be used for good."

"Did you try to sell them?"

"No, I was afraid they would end up in the wrong hands. Honestly, I made them because I enjoyed it. When I wasn't pushing out swords and knives to sell, I took time to work on the art of it all. It was calming and soothing to just sit and mold, to make something that had meant a lot to me when I was a kid. I could never be like the Turtles, but I could provide something that would allow others to be like them. That was what I had to settle for, so in my free time I made something that I dreamt of one day being able to use. I guess you could call it my hobby, in a way. I didn't really have anything else in my life."

"We all have hobbies," Mamacita said, calmly taking off her suit jacket. "And I like the sais very much."

She ripped her long silk sleeves from her shirt one at a time, and tossed them to the side. She stretched her arms over her head and closed her eyes, breathing deeply in and out. The girls looked at her and quieted down, watching every move she made.

"May I use your knife?" She held out a hand to Joshua.

He handed it to her carefully, and she smiled to see the beautiful craftmanship of the blade and handle. She winked at him as she leaned down and cut slits in her expensive skirt all the way to the tops of her thighs.

The girls looked confused, but continued to watch her as she handed the knife back to Joshua and squatted before kicking high in the air.

She turned to the girls and smiled.

"Makes it a whole lot easier to kick without the skirt

holding me in so tight," she explained. "We all have secrets; pasts that we don't often talk about, and dreams that were never fulfilled. Most people have this inner need to protect the ones they love. To push them and make them grow, but sometimes you inadvertently hold them back." She looked at Joshua. "There isn't a magic answer to any of that. Your mother did what she thought was best. But do you know the beauty of it all?"

"What?" Joshua asked.

"You are now a man. A man who is capable of anything he puts his mind to," she told him. "So, if you are ready to be a warrior, then you *can* be one. If you are a weapons master, then you can be that too. Just like I told you the other day...you can be many things, but there is usually only one you are a master of."

Mamacita turned to the side and the girls all gasped. Wrapped around her thigh, disappearing under her skirt, and reappearing across her neck and over her shoulder was a beautiful and intricate dragon tattoo. She had gone to great lengths to hide the tattoo, but for what reason?

The girls had no idea.

She looked like a different woman now, someone they didn't recognize as their former keeper. There had been a secret warrior hidden away under the layers of clothing, long curled hair, and makeup that hid the stories in her eyes.

At that moment, though, as she walked carefully across the floor and kicked off her heels, they saw a different woman. One with honor and respect, one with a past she had yet to reveal, and one who was simmering an idea in her head while they were locked in that basement to wait for a resolution.

"And what are *you* the master of?" Joshua asked.

"Me?" Mamacita laughed. "Well, I'm the master of my own life, I guess. I am good at a lot of things; a lot more things that I let anyone know. But a master? I am not really sure yet."

"Caretaker," one of the girls yelled.

"Aw, that's sweet. I think I am pretty good at that." She smiled. "But not a *master*."

"Businesswoman?" Joshua offered.

"Again, I am really, really good with business." She shrugged. "I am, but I don't think I am a master of that either. I think that what I am a master of hasn't come to me yet, and that's okay. The beauty in life is the journey to find what you are master of. But you know something? I am pretty good at a couple of things you would not have guessed, which was my intent."

Mamacita walked back to the cabinet and carefully pulled the sais from their hooks, then gripped them tightly in her hands as she smiled at Joshua.

They felt right. It was as if she had never ever put them down. She walked forward, twisting one way, then the other, and back again.

Her movements were quick, hard, and structured, like she had performed them all her life. She started to work the sai in her right hand, moving it in circles across her body and back.

When she switched to the left, she fumbled the weapon and it fell to the floor, clanging on the concrete.

She winced. "I guess if someone hasn't practiced in a

few years, you can't expect perfection right away," She picked it up and returned to her place.

"You know how to use those?" Joshua asked in wonder.

She didn't look at him, just nodded. "I sure do, Joshua," She smiled, moving into the traditional *heisoku dachi* stance.

She bent slowly forward, bowing to Joshua before making a hard turn and bowing to the girls. She moved from the formal attention stance quickly into the *nicho sai*.

Her hand, holding the sai, snapped up and behind her head, while she tucked her other sai to her side, tip towards her back.

She slowly moved her front leg, dragging her toe around in a half moon in front of her self before calling out as she front punched, once, twice, and a third time. She then shifted back into the *nicho sai* again, holding still for a moment.

From there she danced across the room, showing the girls her beautiful art.

"*Iyaaa*," she yelled, chopping one hand down into her leg, holding her pose perfectly as if she had done it her whole life.

She incorporated the sais into her *kata*, swinging them around, twirling them through her hands, and flowing from pose to pose without hesitation.

She began to sweat as she moved, completely focused inward. Her muscles tensed and relaxed, their definition visible for the first time in a very long time.

The girls were entranced, unable to move or talk.

Joshua was having a hard time understanding or believing the talent the woman had hidden from everyone.

Slowly she flowed back into the beginning stance and breathed out deeply, bowing to Joshua and then to the girls, who gamely tried to bow back to her. She stood up straight and opened her eyes, smiling around the room.

There was no sound at all in the basement—just the presence of the girls, of Joshua, and of Mamacita.

"You see, ladies...and Joshua," Mamacita began, "sometimes you have to stop running from your past to make sure those you love have a *future.*"

Joshua didn't understand what she meant and neither did the girls, really, but they all understood her intent. *They* were the ones she loved, the ones she wanted to have a future.

They watched as she walked to the large door leading to the tunnel and slowly turned the lock. As it clanked open, she gripped the sais and looked back at the group.

"If I never am blessed to see you again, know that I'll watch over you from heaven," she told them, a sad smile gracing her face.

She turned back to the door and opened it, then slid into the hallway and closed the door behind her. Joshua's smile faded when he realized she was going to fight the demons.

He wouldn't let her fight alone.

"Take a weapon," Joshua said, and the girls walked up to the cabinet one by one. "Hold it tightly in your hand. Feel it as part of you. Know that where it goes, you go. When you strike, aim for the face, the neck, or the chest, but try to stay back. I've seen these beasts' claws, and they are *brutal*."

"You think we are ready?" one of the girls asked Joshua.

"If you think you are ready, then you are," he told her, giving her shoulder a tiny squeeze. "You are the bravest women I have ever met, and you were fighting demons long before Korbin's Killers started. They just came to you in other forms."

They all lined up as the he opened the door, then looked back at them and lifted his sword into the air. They shouted and cheered loudly before running full-force through the door and down the tunnel.

When they reached the end, there were two demons blocking their path. The front two girls lurched forward and swiped their weapons across the demons' skin. Mad with pain and agony, the demons lashed out, severely injuring both women.

Joshua shouted and ran toward the demons, wielding his weapons like a true master. He fought the beasts, injuring them repeatedly. He kicked them, slashed them with his blade, and finally knocked them backward into the wall of the cave.

The boy surprised them. They hadn't seen or heard of him before tonight.

Joshua could feel the anger surging through him, which was new to him. He had to protect the women.

His mind was clear, and he could see every move before he performed it.

He sliced down through one of the demon's heads, splitting it open. That one fell to the ground as he turned and slashed his sword across the remaining demon's chest, blood splattering to the ground.

He raced forward, cutting through the second demon's claws as he pulled a knife from the sheath on his belt. The demon had frozen and was screaming at the pain of losing a hand.

Joshua lunged forward and stabbed the knife deep into the demon's chest, piercing its dark black heart. The demon gurgled and spat until finally it died. Joshua pushed the beast off his knife and watched as it turned to dust just before hitting the ground.

"You don't think a blacksmith knows how to FIGHT?" he screamed at the pile of demon ash.

Two of the women had pulled the injured to safety, and began treating their wounds. The girls nodded to Joshua, and Joshua to them. He couldn't believe he had possibly lost two of his girls in the first thirty seconds of the fight.

In that moment he started to question his decision to equip the girls to fight with him, but as he watched the others attack he smiled, seeing a warrior in each and every one of them. They were no longer just flesh for sale.

And he was no longer just a lonely weapons maker.

They were part of something bigger than themselves. He had given them a reason to fight, and work, and train, and believe. They had entered into something that would change them forever—but in a good way, a way that might keep them from entering that brothel ever again.

Korbin, Calvin, Jeremy, and Derek surrounded one of the larger demons, their weapons at the ready.

This fucker had huge muscles, rows of jagged teeth, and scaly skin so thick barely anything could penetrate it.

The demon turned toward Korbin and roared, shaking the walls of the base. Derek took a running start and leapt onto the beast's back, slicing it across the back of the neck. The beast bucked and screamed loudly in pain, and reached back to grab Derek. It tossed him hard, sending him flying through the air to crash into a wall.

He groaned as he fell to the ground, grabbing his arm tightly, then pulled himself up and looked at the others.

"My arm…it's broken. I'll shoot from here. I won't get in the way!"

The others nodded and turned back toward the beast, sending shots winging toward the demon. Derek pulled out his pistol with his left hand and aimed at the beast's face, pulling the trigger until his clip was empty.

The beast growled but ignored the bullets and Derek looked down, trying to reload his weapon with one hand. One of the bullets dropped from the clip and he bent down, cussing as he tried to get the damn thing to load.

"Derek," Jeremy yelled to him. "Watch out!"

Derek looked up to see Jeremy sprinting toward him with his sword out, then glanced over his shoulder to see a demon very close. He dropped to the ground and scooted backward as the demon crept toward him.

Jeremy lunged forward to shove the sword through the demon's shoulder, then pulled hard to remove it—but it was stuck. He looked up at the demon, kicking it to hopefully pull the sword free. Then he turned his head toward Derek, eyes wide, and his expression went blank.

Derek looked down to see the demon's talons pushing through the kid's stomach and out the other side.

"NOOOO!" Derek screamed as the demon retracted his claws. Jeremy, with no support, fell slowly to the ground, his eyes dimming.

Derek got his other pistol free and pointed it at the demon's face, pulling the trigger until its clip had run dry as well. He continued to pull, the clicks echoing through his head, as anger overtook him. He looked down at Jeremy's body and gritted his teeth.

"Why the fuck would you do that?" he screamed at his dead teammate. "You are paying your *tribute* too fucking early!"

Derek stood there and watched as the demon turned to dust, Jeremy's sword falling to the ground and clanging on the pavement. Behind him Korbin and Calvin double-teamed their demon, making serious headway with injuring the big-assed bastard.

However, as Calvin stepped forward to swipe at the demon again, it swung its large arm outward and caught Calvin, sending him tumbling ass over appetite across the ground. He moaned as he heard his bones cracking.

"I'll just be a second," he called weakly from the sidelines.

A female's arm came into view. "You tap out for a moment," Mamacita told him, pressing her hand on Calvin's arm as she looked toward the demon. "I've got Korbin's back."

"Well, all right." Calvin chuckled and turned his head to spit out blood, surprised to see her.

Mamacita headed into the fight and nodded at Korbin as she stepped up next to him, her sais gripped tightly in her hands.

He returned the nod and looked back at the demon, who was laughing menacingly.

Korbin's lip twitched in irritation.

"You are so badly beaten that now you have to bring in *girls*?" The demon chuckled deeply.

"I wouldn't judge a book by its cover," Mamacita told it, moving forward in an intricate pattern. Her sais twirled in the air before she stabbed one of them into the demon's side and moved back.

The beast yelled in agony, falling to its knees and grabbing its side. There was something about the sai that bothered it more than the other weapons had.

It slid in like a motherfucker.

The two humans started to fight in earnest again, causing the beast damage so grave that Korbin was eventually able to cut its head off. He climbed off the body and went over to Mamacita, both hurt and walking poorly.

Korbin shook his head and chuckled, just happy to have had some help.

———

Katie stood close to Eric and Damian as they fought two large sneaky demons. One was faster and thinner, while the other one was pure brute. Eric ran toward the skinny beast and jinked to the right as his knife sliced across its stomach, but the blade caught a claw on the other side and he had to pull back.

He realized it was just a flesh wound, so he retreated.

Katie and Damian continued to attack, both getting hit pretty hard in the process. Katie was still holding her own, though, no matter what the demon threw at her.

"These fuckers are a mess," Katie said, rubbing her bruised arm.

"Hell yeah they are," Eric said, shaking his head and breathing heavily. "I have a secret weapon, though."

Eric walked over to the large pieces of concrete wall that had fallen during the battle. He groaned as he lifted one into the air, but once it was up he closed his eyes and stepped back, putting out his hands. With a telekinetic effort, he threw the stone harder than he would ever be able to do with his own hands.

The rock flew through the air and bashed into the demon, which got its attention. The demon turned quickly and snarled at Eric, and he slowly pulled his two knives from their sheaths and held them behind his back.

The demon lunged forward, not paying attention as Eric held a knife out. The demon ran straight into it and screamed in pain, stumbling backward as Eric reared back and threw the other one into the demon's shoulder.

The beast's screeches of pain echoed around the compound.

Eric smiled at the screams, knowing how much pain he had inflicted.

Before he could react, though, the demon pulled the knife from his shoulder and threw it at Eric, striking him back in the arm. Eric screamed and fell to the ground himself.

The knife did its fair share of damage, but what was really damaging was that the metal—the special metal made to hurt the demons —absolutely scrambled Eric's demon's brain.

Eric writhed on the ground for a moment before pulling the knife out of his arm.

Pandora growled as she watched the scene through Katie's eyes, then turned back to the two demons. The faster one stood at the front and was attempting to stare Pandora down, growling, snarling, and getting ready to attack.

Before it could, though, the larger demon crept up behind it and grabbed the first by the shoulders, swinging it around to face him. He shoved his hand into the demon's chest and ripped out its heart, popping the organ into his mouth and chomping away.

Oh, man, Pandora said. *This is gonna suck.*

How badly? Katie asked, in shock from the cannibalistic action happening right in front of her.

On a scale of one to shove-a-tree-up-my-ass? Pandora replied. *I'll take the tree every time.*

That's...pretty bad, Katie agreed.

The smaller demon fell to the ground, its body slowly melting into the concrete.

She winced, wondering how that felt before looking back up at the remaining demon.

The brute demon growled and howled. Its muscles pulsating and increased in size as it grew taller, and its skin glowed brighter by the second.

Katie looked at Damian, who was kneeling next to Eric and wrapping his wounds. As he treated Eric, he kept an eye on the demon.

"Well," Damian remarked, "this is a horrible new ability to learn about on the killing field."

"You got this." Eric winced as he shook his head. "You and Katie are badasses, so you shouldn't even be worried about that fucker. He may be big, but hey...you can tell he's as dumb as a box of fucking rocks."

"Thanks for that." Damian smiled. "Nice pep talk."

He patted Eric on the arm, then stood up and walked over to Katie. She seemed to be completely and totally in shock.

He chuckled as he watched the demon. "It looks like they've got all kinds of tricks up their sleeves," he pondered aloud. "Wish we had a list of their abilities.

"Yeah, maybe they have a few tricks," she said. "But so...do...we."

We're really going to do this? Pandora asked. *No going back afterwards.*

Do it.

Katie walked forward with her eyes flashing bright red and Pandora brewing inside of her. The beast turned its head and stared at Katie, who had no fear in her heart.

A sick smile moved over its lips as it crouched, ready for action.

"DRESS REHEARSAL FOR HELL, BOYS!" Pandora and Katie yelled in unison.

Katie put her hands out in front of her and watched as they slowly morphed into demonic paws with long sharp claws. When she looked up, her eyes were nothing but bright red orbs, and two red horns sprouted from the top of her head. She growled and seethed as she stared up at the beast.

"Well," Damian said, looking at her in disbelief, "that is definitely a new tactic."

He looked her up and down as her clothes ripped and shredded. Her body became wider, taller and stronger than her human form. She had grown huge; taller than him, her arm muscles glistening from the sweat rolling down her skin. She looked at Damian and winked, a smile moving across her lips.

"Don't worry, I'm still me," she said, reaching her hand out for Damian's cross. "There is just *more* of me."

Damian nodded and removed the cross from his jacket. He paused before slapping the cross into her hands, but it had no effect on her. He shook his head, not sure what to think about her metamorphosis.

"Go take care of Eric," she bellowed. "That lazy fucker isn't going to die on my watch."

Eric's sputtering voice called, "I got your lazy right here! Leave that sumbitch for me. I'll drive my sword up its ass and shit down its throat."

Damian nodded to Katie and turned to Eric, but looked over his shoulder to catch another glimpse of Katie. This was wholly new to him.

Katie shoved the cross into her belt and stepped onto the fallen stone, looking over at the beast. She lunged forward and plowed into the beast, pushing it through the wall and sending it sliding across the ground on the other side. Bricks fell all over them as they traveled.

The two slashed back and forth, throwing large sections of wall and old equipment from the unused area of the compound. The fight was vicious, and caused widespread damage to the empty buildings.

As they wrestled for the upper hand, small fires erupted from the heat of their bodies colliding. They destroyed several of the buildings, but they didn't stop.

Katie was not going to allow this demon to get away or hurt anyone else.

"Hey, fucker," Pandora called from within Katie. "Just give up, you piece of shit. T'Chezz is going to kill you anyway."

"Fuck you," he roared, lunging at Katie.

Katie put her feet beneath his hips and rolled backward, pushing him into the air. She got out of the way as he plummeted back to the ground, crushing the concrete beneath him when he landed. Slowly he got himself back onto his feet, and dusted his hands off on his massive scaly legs.

He smiled again, shaking his head.

"There isn't anything you can do that I don't know about," the demon said to Pandora. "I can do this all day and all night up here on Earth. You are nothing like you are in Hell—just an empty shell of your former self—but I have been infused with power to last weeks, maybe even longer."

"Take me over there," Katie told Pandora. "Nobody talks to my friend like this jackass."

Pandora laughed and the two of them ran toward the sack of shit, tackling the demon again and smashing through the support columns of the nearest building.

She slashed her paws back and forth, the claws sinking deep into the beast's flesh. He roared in pain when Katie and Pandora pinned him to the floor beneath them. Katie tightened her legs around him and straddled him, looking down into his eyes.

This time only the human's voice emerged.

"You fucking waste of demon flesh," Katie hissed. "Pandora might have lost some of her powers, but she has gained more than you could fucking *imagine*."

Katie lifted her right arm, and her human hand returned. She chuckled and grabbed the cross from her belt. She held it up, her face a reflection in the smooth metal.

"Choke on this, you goat-licking bag of dick tips," Katie screamed as she shoved the cross through the demon's teeth into the back of his mouth.

She slid forward onto his chest and pinned his arms,

then jammed his chin closed as he gagged from the cross lodged in his throat.

He moaned in agony, and thrashed to try to knock her off. Katie groaned as he rolled around in panic, breaking a couple of her ribs and possibly her knee, but she held on for dear life.

After several minutes and a fucking huge amount of pain for both of them, the demon's head began to melt.

His body finally went limp, only twitching from time to time, so Katie stood up and moved to the side.

She stared as his flesh begin to liquify. His head glowed with the golden light from the cross, and she waited until he was completely gone before moving.

She slowly walked over and stared down, then pulled up her shredded sleeve and reached down into the goo to pick up the cross.

Ewww, Pandora wailed. *Don't you wipe that shit off on us. No fucking way!*

Katie found an old love seat pushed against the wall, so she walked over and wiped the cross as clean as she could, then held it up and shrugged. In the other area, Damian and Eric stopped to listen for any sound, but could hear nothing.

"Okay," Eric said, sitting up. "What's going on? There are no explosions, no yelling, no earth-shattering falls."

"I don't know," Damian admitted, standing up.

As he was about to go check the large sliding metal door to the building creaked open. Damian got into his stance, his sword at the ready, waiting to see who was coming out.

He slowly began to relax as Katie turned the corner,

now normal-sized. What was left of her clothes barely covered her body.

She walked toward Damian and Eric with a smirk on her face. As she drew closer, she pulled out the cross and tossed it up and down a couple of times.

When she reached Damian, she tossed it to him.

"That fucker choked on it."

After a change of clothes Katie, Korbin, and Calvin decided to scope out the damage, so they made their way to the roof.

Katie sat down on the edge and dangled her legs over, watching as Korbin sat down on one side of her and Calvin on the other. The place was smashed: buildings demolished, walls crumbling, power lines down and sparking. It looked like a war zone around there. It was mildly depressing.

Katie scrunched her nose and leaned back on her hands.

"Sorry about demolishing your other buildings," Katie said.

Korbin sighed. "It's all par for the course. To be honest, this place is just not safe anymore. The demons know where we are, and if we don't leave, they will just keep coming back until we are all dead. They took one of us tonight, one of us who deserved a lot more time on this

Earth and on this team, and we can't afford to lose anyone else. I can't take it, and I won't allow it."

"I know you want to protect us, boss," Katie told him. "But you have to remember that this is our life, and it will be all of our deaths at some point or the other. I agree we need to move on from here, but I can't let you take responsibility for our deaths. You are not accountable for us, and you need to stop letting yourself fall into that pit."

"That is easier said than done, kid." Korbin sighed, then stood and walked around. "When you are the leader, you are responsible for your team—alive *and* dead."

Katie nodded and looked down at the ground below. "Where to now?"

"Don't know." Korbin replied. "I just know we need to move. Joshua and the others, they almost got stuck in our fucking war. That was more than irresponsible of me. It was *reckless*."

"We need to find another safe haven," Calvin added. "Somewhere we can feel comfortable laying our heads down at night. Where we can train and get ready for the next time this happens. I just don't know where we can go, you know?"

"I think we all need to stay together," Katie said. "Splitting up the team—and that includes Joshua, who killed four demons during the fight—would be bad; really bad for us. One of the reasons we work so damn well together is because we are each other's family. If we split up, we'll lose our familiarity and bond with each other. I don't want to fight with a stranger who looks like Korbin, I want to fight with my brothers. I want to know they have my back and I have theirs…and that is something that we all have, including Joshua."

"I don't know what to do, Katie." Korbin looked around at the damage. "I need a day to let my brain settle. Right now all I can see is that battle and Jeremy's body. I am not in a good place at this moment to make a long-term decision like that."

"Knock, knock," Mamacita called from behind them.

Katie turned around. "Hey."

She smiled. "Hey there, pretty girl,"

"I heard you were one badass bitch today," Katie told her, rolling her feet back over the wall and standing up to hug her. "Thank you for being there for us; for putting your life in danger for all this. We couldn't have made it through without you."

"Aw, you would have been fine," She smiled and kissed Katie on the cheek.

Korbin looked at her and noticed that she had changed. She was no longer dressed in a suit or wearing robes in the brothel. She was just wearing normal clothes.

Her hair was straight and pulled back at the nape of her neck, not up and wild like she usually wore it. It was refreshing to see her that way—just a regular woman for once.

"I have to say," Mamacita began as she walked over and sat down on the ledge, "I was a little misinformed."

"Why do you say that?" Calvin asked.

"Well, what you guys do and what I *thought* you did are very different," she admitted, chuckling. "It was definitely a new experience."

"Yeah," Korbin snapped at her. "An experience you

should *never* have been a part of. You could have been killed, dammit! You were supposed to stay down there with those girls to keep them calm and protect them, not come bolting up the tunnel like a wild karate master, trying to take down demons you know nothing about."

"I deal with *you* every day, don't I?" Mamacita snapped back.

"Not the same. You could have died in a heartbeat!" He sighed, rubbing his face and calming his voice before he spoke again. "We did lose someone, and we almost lost two of your girls, too. I don't understand why you aren't taking this seriously."

She turned her head slightly to look at him. "I *am*! Why do you think I risked my ass to come topside and fight that nasty-ass crusty demon with you?" she retorted. "It definitely wasn't for the hell of it, that's for sure."

Korbin sighed, wiping his face. "Well, I have to admit that your moves were damned impressive. I had no idea you had anything like that in you." He mumbled something that sounded like an apology.

"I didn't learn to fight overnight," she told him, picking up a stone and looking down at her hands. "I trained in martial arts until my early twenties. That was when I ran from the cult, and please make no mistake about it—it *was* a damned cult."

"Is that how you ended up at the house?" Katie asked.

"Yeah, sort of," Mamacita replied. "I am the niece of the original owner of the house, and I worked really hard to make it a place where girls could go when they didn't feel like they belonged or didn't have a family to help support them. I wanted to give girls another option than just going into an empty marriage, being homeless, or joining a gang. Perhaps my option was not that great. Maybe it was immoral or a bad choice, but it was all I knew. When I was out on my own, sex was how I stayed alive. It paid for my food every night, and a hotel room most nights. Over time, it became a business; something I could rely on, get an apartment with. Then I took over the house, and that was when I realized I had the opportunity to help other women. So I did."

"And how do you feel about it now?" Korbin asked.

She chuckled and shook her head. "Now that I see the reality of the world, I can't go back to that. Actually, it's more like I *won't* go back. My life has been a beautiful thing since I met you guys, from Armani originally to these business opportunities to watching the girls grow and forming friendships. I learned about the world in a way I never thought I would, and I cannot just walk away from that."

Korbin shook his head and sighed, raking his hands through his hair. He didn't know what to say, since he didn't want to put Mamacita in harm's way—not even for a second.

But at the same time, she really only had two options at that point. It was the rule, no matter who it was. She knew the truth, as did those girls, and that was going to hurt the Killers if they didn't follow guidelines. He turned back to her and put his hands by his sides.

"There are only two options, Mamacita—"

"My name is Stephanie Lee," she interrupted, watching them eye her. "I had mixed parents. My mom is Hispanic, which is where I get my dark skin and dark hair. It's also where I get my damn temper."

"Well, that makes sense now," Calvin agreed, nodding.

She shrugged. "My dad, he was calm, and always about the body and his martial arts."

"We are going to have to leave here," Korbin told her. "This place is not safe for anyone, and I don't just mean because of the construction zone. We are now on the map for the demons, and I know if they are given a shot they will come back here and finish us off. I don't want to give them that shot. We can split up for now—go over to other teams—or I can start looking for a good piece of property, or we can become Korbin's Homeless Killers."

"You know," Stephanie mused. "I actually might have a solution. I have some property with a large building on it on the northeast side of town. It's about forty-five minutes from here, out toward Area 51. We could set everything up there like it was here."

"That's really sweet of you," Korbin said, "but trust me, you've done enough. Believe it or not, our project—this whole thing—is even more secretive than Area 51. If we were to move over in that direction and end up in another firefight like the last one, I can guarantee that the Feds would start bitching. They are supposed to be protecting the oh-so-precious Area 51. Besides, I think that it's finally time that we just bite the bullet, no pun intended, and build a full-out war base. Something that is hidden and can be heavily fortified, and will be around for a long time. We need our own airfield and our own transportation on call, and we need to feel safe and secure at the place we call home."

"Can we have a tank?" Katie asked.

He chuckled. "Sure."

"Then I might be okay with it, as long as I don't have to wear a uniform," Katie replied.

"No, no uniforms," he said, shaking his head. "Just safety—that's all I'm saying. Bunkers for nights like this. Places where we can hide out and be safe, or hide the people we care about. I don't want to keep burying people because we aren't prepared. We should have been prepared for something like what happened. It was crazy not to think they would come looking for us, but I just let it slip my mind—and then there they were, knocking on our front door."

"We were preparing the place." Katie waved a hand around. "We just weren't fast enough."

"And that isn't an excuse," he answered softly. "Anyway, I need to get some work done."

"And I need some sleep," Stephanie said.

Katie waited until Korbin and Calvin had said goodnight and disappeared back into the building before she turned to Stephanie.

"Are you really *determined* to fight?" Katie asked, one eyebrow raised.

She pursed her lips, nodded her head, and walked off without another word.

The next morning, Katie woke up ready to get her day started. She couldn't seem to get Mamacita off her mind—and the reaction that Korbin was having toward her.

She got dressed and headed down to Korbin's office, determined to make him talk about it; to find out why he was pushing Mamacita—or rather, Stephanie—away so hard.

When she got to the main area, Eric and Derek were sitting in the living room thinking about the service they wanted to have for Jeremy. They asked for her input, but she had none.

Katie felt strange about it. Obviously she was sad, but she was also numb—as if there wasn't a reason for her to grieve. She thought that if she started, she would be grieving the losses of her friends forever.

At the same time, she knew that eventually it would come up in her mind. She just assumed she wasn't ready for it.

"Hey." Katie knocked on the doorframe when she reached Korbin's office.

"Hey," he said.

"Can I come in?"

"Sure," he replied, leaning back in his chair. "What's up?"

"Are you going to let Mamaci—I'm sorry, *Stephanie*—join our team?" Katie asked.

"Close the door, please," he said, nodding at it.

She shut the door as she entered and sat down in front of him. He stayed quiet for several moments, mulling Katie's question. Katie could tell he wanted to say something, but wasn't sure he should.

After the silence became too much, Katie spoke up.

"You can tell me the truth. Like, the real truth. I'm old enough, Dad."

He chuckled. "I know. I'm worried that my feelings for her are messing up my decision-making process."

"Ahh, I see." Katie smiled. "So because of that, you're going to be a dick and choose something for her that goes against what she actually wants. Right. Got it."

"No, not necessarily," he admitted. "I'm conflicted."

"It's not like she didn't prove herself," Katie pointed out. "She's already made her choice, but you are blocking her from joining the fight. I just don't get it! We need strong, capable people on the team, and she *wants* this."

"She's not even *Damned*," Korbin retorted. "And this would be her whole life."

"So? It's *her* decision," Katie replied. "What are you going to do, wipe her memories?"

"You can still do that, right?" Korbin asked, eyeing her nervously.

"Really?" She sighed, rolling her eyes. "Yes, I can do that. But please, Korbin, don't make me."

While Katie and Korbin talked in the office, the rest of the house was quiet. Some were mourning, others planning their next steps, but the sounds of happiness and joy were gone.

The last thing Katie wanted to do was remove someone's memories, especially someone she cared about. Several minutes later she came out of Korbin's office and closed the door behind her. As she made her way to the elevator, Pandora finally popped her head out.

So, I think today should be a soaps-and-game-show day, she said. *We both kicked ass, and it's time to relax.*

That actually sounds really nice, Katie replied. *But unfortunately, we don't have time to do that right now. We have been given a job.*

Ugh, Pandora grumped. *We are always doing something. Why can't we just chill out and be done with it?*

Katie chuckled. *Soon. How about this: I'll get you some donuts.*

Fucking deal, Pandora agreed. *Wait, how many is "some?"*

I don't know, like two?

Make it three, and it's a deal, Pandora told her.

You got it. She laughed.

Katie pushed the button for the headlights, but instead the windshield wipers came on. She turned the knob frantically to try to stop them while still paying attention to the road.

It was late morning so she didn't need the lights, but it was an old habit her mom instilled in her when she was first starting to drive. Finally she got the wipers off, and decided that was enough playing around for one car ride.

She put both hands on the steering wheel and focused on the drive to Mamacita's house in Las Vegas.

She had a mission to carry out, and she needed to concentrate on that. However, every time she glanced at the seat next to her, all she could think about was her Ferrari.

Goddamn this fucking SUV, Katie bitched. *I want my car back. I paid a lot for it and I really loved it, and your fucking brother took it back to hell with him. He doesn't deserve a vehicle that sophisticated and fine. And God, I paid for it in CASH. It's not like I had insurance on the sonofabitch. All I wanted was something nice of my own, and I was fucking robbed.*

Okay, and what may I ask would you have put down on the form when it asked you for the reason for the claim? "Drove car to hell can't get it back?"

Maybe, Katie said with irritation. *Or that it was stolen, even. I could have reported it stolen.*

And had the cops come take a statement at the base, where the walls are falling down and there is demon ash everywhere? Pandora asked. *Besides, I overheard the payouts for these different demons. Seriously, another big one and we can move on up to that Aston Martin Vanquish Volante, like in a sweet sparkly black and shit.*

So I can get it smashed to hell? Katie scoffed. *No thanks.*

And then, Pandora continued, ignoring her negative comment, *when we take out my fucktard of a brother, we can go for the 918 Spyder Hybrid and still have enough money left over to do whatever you want. He is worth some real cash, woman. I was surprised, since he is the same level as me. I am fucking pricey.*

At least his ass will be worth something in my lifetime, Katie grumped. *He can pay me back for the car with his fucking life.*

That's morbid, Pandora responded, waiting a moment before adding, *"I like it."*

Katie pulled up to the gate at the house and rolled down the window. She reached out and pressed the call button, waiting for someone to answer.

She looked down at her nails and sighed, figuring there was no point in a manicure if she was constantly punching demons in the face.

"Hello?" the girl on the other end answered.

"Hey, it's Katie," she said.

"Come on up," the girl said cheerfully.

The gates slowly opened, and Katie pulled through and around the circle to the front of the house. She sat there for a second, still stewing over her car. She just couldn't stop being so bitter about it.

You sure have gotten comfortable with this place, Pandora told her. *Am I finally getting you comfortable with your sexuality?*

No, Katie said flatly. *But we kicked ass together, and I won't disrespect them by thinking of them as anything less than equals.*

You sure? Pandora picked at her. *Not even the slightest bit? You never think about big dic—*

Stop, please God, Katie groaned, getting out of the car.

Well, I'm not the Big Guy, but if you want to pray to me... No? I thought I would try it. It's the least I can do.

When Katie got to the front door one of the girls, Alice, was already opening the front door.

She smiled and gave Katie a big hug. Katie wasn't really a hugger, but she knew the girls had been through a lot. She wasn't going to be that person who acted like an ass about a hug.

Katie walked inside and looked around, noticing that the place was very empty.

"Where is everyone?" Katie asked.

"Oh, most of the girls are at the hospital visiting the two who got hurt," she said sadly. "And Mamacita will be back in a few minutes. She went out to do something."

"How are the girls?" Katie asked.

"They are both doing okay," she said. "Battered, bruised, and stitched up, but nothing any of us haven't been through before with our own personal brand of demons."

Katie smiled sadly. "I'm sorry. I wish you guys had been protected."

"We chose to fight," the girl shot back. "We wanted to stand up and be strong."

"Well, you did. Now, you said she won't be home for a couple of minutes?"

"Yeah," Alice replied.

"Okay, that's perfect. It will allow us to find what we need."

About ten minutes later, Katie heard Mamacita coming in the front door. She popped her head out and smiled, watching her carrying a couple of shopping bags into the house. She was wearing new clothes, ones that fit her a lot better than before.

She was dressed in wide-legged black dress pants, black and white Chuck Taylors, a sleeveless black shirt, and a pair of rimmed sunglasses with large lenses. Her tats were visible, too. She didn't seem to have anything left of the old her at all.

She smiled as Katie walked around the corner. "Hey, Katie! What are you doing here?"

"I came at Korbin's request, and I need to speak with you privately, if you don't mind," Katie answered.

"Sure, come on back to my old office," she said, nodding toward the back.

Everything looked different; even the sitting area was sleeker and less Victorian. Katie felt a lot more comfortable with it like this.

She sat down across from Stephanie, who had chosen to sit on her couch and put her hands in her lap.

"So, I came to talk to you about what being Damned means," Katie said. "I know that it looks all glamorous and stuff, but it's tough."

Stephanie snorted.

"Ok, maybe not 'glamorous.' You have to give up your whole life, you train your ass off every day, you have to go when called, you may or may not have a responsive demon in you, and there is always a chance that your demon could take control, which means you would have to be killed."

"Okay," she said with a small laugh. "So sunshiny and bright you always are, my dear Katie."

"Beyond the fact that you have to give up your life and everyone in it, there is a rule," Katie said. "When you become infected, you are given one of three choices: death, research, or exorcism—or of course the team. I guess that's four choices, really."

Stephanie pondered her words for a moment.

"Research?"

"You *are* the research, so it really isn't much of an option. That puts us back to three... Kinda one, if I think about it. Who is going to choose death?"

Stephanie thought about it a moment before responding, "You know what I really hate? I hate the fact that Korbin is having any damn say in this at all. It should be completely *my* choice, whether I am Damned or not. Seriously, it should be mine. I guess I can't do anything about that, so if it's going to be a man making my choices, I suppose it's not too bad that Korbin is that man."

Katie smiled. "I suppose not. If you choose to do this, what will happen to the house and the girls?"

Stephanie looked around. "Oh, I'm not in the prostitution business anymore. I closed that down as soon as I got back," she admitted. "In reality, we have been tapering down ever since you started that company and we helped out over there. I signed a contract this morning for an organization to turn this place into a halfway house. I put a clause in the contract that gives the house to the organization if I should randomly die, so whether I change or not, that is going to happen."

Katie stared at her for a moment with her mouth open before her mind caught up and she closed it. "Wow, that's really...wow...generous of you," Katie said. "What about the girls? Where will they go?"

"Well, Joshua has offered everyone a job," she replied. "Most are actually taking him up on it, and the ones that aren't, they are moving back with their families. I checked if those girls had good home lives and they do, so I am satisfied with all of that. That means if I change I still get to see most of my girls, which was the majority of my life anyway."

"So, is that your choice?" Katie asked. "Do you want to be infected?"

"Well, when you put it that way..." She smiled, her eyes a bit distant before she focused on Katie. "Yes, I do."

Katie nodded, cocking her head to the right. "Did you know that there are a couple of succubi living in this house?" she asked scooting up in her chair to get closer to Stephanie.

"No. What do they do?" she asked, her eyes narrowing.

"Well, they use whatever sexual energy they need, and then they send all sorts of energy back into the house to keep everyone aroused," Katie explained.

Stephanie laughed. "No wonder I had such a good business here."

"I caught the strongest one, and figured it was time to put her to some real work," Katie said.

Katie leaned forward, opened her mouth, and blew in Stephanie's direction. The succubus came out, screaming in fear at having spent the last twenty minutes with Pandora.

Katie shook her head and laughed.

That succubus is a serious PRUDE, Pandora bitched. *Hell, I was teaching* her *shit!*

Pandora let go of her and the succubus sped forward, slamming into Mamacita. She gasped and looked at Katie, who was smiling widely. Mamacita tilted her head from side to side in confusion.

"Welcome to the Damned," Katie said as her new teammate fell over on the couch, out cold. "As Damian would say, 'It gets them every time.'"

Yeah, it does, Pandora chuckled. *It's cute. Really, it is.*

Okay, I need you to give me some extra strength, Katie said. *I'm kind of sore, and I need to carry her out to the car.*

You got it, Mama, Pandora said.

And please don't make me a giant again. It worked for that situation, but it's overkill for this one, Katie requested.

Okay, she griped.

Katie took a moment to let Alice know she was taking Mamacita with her before returning to the office.

She leaned down and picked Stephanie up off the couch

and sighed. She didn't remember passing out when she'd gotten Pandora, but then again, she had been chained in an old parking garage.

It hadn't really been a good situation in which to fall unconscious.

She remembered Garrett's face as he'd wheeled her out to the SUV and taken her back to the base. It had been the beginning of some really good things, and now Katie was getting to do that for Stephanie.

She opened the side door of the SUV and put her in the seat, buckling her in for safety. She pulled the straps tight and leaned her head back.

"Welcome to Korbin's Killers, Stephanie," she whispered, closing the door, walking around the front of the vehicle, and hopping in the driver's seat.

The crowd was rowdy at the bar Torn Asunder, laughing, talking, and reconnecting since the last special night they'd had. Katie was going to start off the night again by talking about Jeremy and reading what they had now dubbed as "the Damned Creed."

She didn't know how she had become the spokesperson, but she didn't mind doing it. It let her pay tribute to her friends and family when they didn't make it through.

Katie looked down at her watch and winked at Damian as she stood up and made her way to the stage. She tapped the mic to get everyone's attention, and smiled as several people cheered for her.

"Thanks for joining us, as always," Katie began, pulling

that old wrinkled piece of paper out of her pocket and unfolding it.

"Before I read the Creed, I want to start off by paying tribute to our fallen brother, Jeremy Croft. He was an FBI agent in his human life, or so I like to call it. In his Damned life he was a hell of a fighter, a friend, and a member of our family. We will miss him, and we hope that wherever he is now, he is having one hell of a time."

Katie raised her glass in the air.

"To Jeremy," she toasted, and everyone repeated his name. "And because I am a person of few words, I will just end this with the Damned Creed.

We are the chosen.
The infected,
battling our demons night and day.
Protecting the uninformed from reality.
We fight where the stupid meet the clueless to
perform the asinine for our
teammates every day.
We are cops, military, special forces, and SWAT,
medical techs, priests, and clergy.
We *are* the dimensional derelicts,
the legion, the host, the forgotten.
The *feared*.
The sheep can sleep at night because we don't.
We fight for humanity—yours—and for our own.
We are the Damned, and death is our enemy,
our escape,
and our *tribute*."

Everyone clapped and cheered, raising their glasses as Katie stepped down off the stage and made her way to the table to join the rest of her team. Stephanie nodded at her and smiled, and the others patted her on the shoulder. Derek handed her a shot.

She held it up in the air.

"To Jeremy," Eric offered.

"To Jeremy," the group replied.

After that they switched up the mood, and had some fun, laughter, and good conversation.

About an hour into it, though, they heard a commotion behind them and Stephanie turned around to check it out. Everyone at the table picked up their food, but Stephanie was too busy watching the fight, commenting on their lack of proper balance as she critiqued their form.

Her eyes grew big as one guy picked the other up and tossed him straight at their table.

Stephanie slid her chair back immediately, putting her arms up in the air as the guy hit the table and it smashed into a pile on the floor—along with her food.

She looked down at the guy and pushed him with her toe, narrowing her eyes at the cheese fries sticking out from under his back. The bartender waved to two others, who moved quickly to grab a table and set it atop the passed-out guy.

Stephanie realized the others had their food in their hands, and they were all staring at her with smiles on their face.

"And that," Korbin told her, setting his food back down. "is why the furniture is in such horrible condition."

AUTHOR NOTES - MICHAEL TODD ANDERLE

WRITTEN MARCH 31, 2018

Want to enjoy some in-between story release fun? Hit us up on Facebook Group and request to join. We will add you just as soon as we see the request! (We have to be on FB to do this.)

http://www.facebook.com/groups/320172985053521/

First, THANK YOU for not only reading our stories, but also reading to our author notes here in the back, as well!

John Kern, Proprietor of Spurlock's Guns in Henderson, is *real*

So, a huge shout-out to John Kern with Spurlock's (http://www.spurlocksguns.com) for helping me understand how to go about properly strategizing what to do with the rounds for Katie and the team.

So, most of this book was finished, and editing and beta reading was happening with one huge issue:

Chapter 17 still needed to be written!

Yes, you read that right, I had a big glaring hole in the middle of the manuscript. My intent was to locate source here in Vegas that I could talk to, and put that information here in the book. Further, I wanted the information for Joshua to be accurate as well so the logic behind the solution.

Finally, if I could I wanted it to be a place fans could look at and realize 'that place is real, that person is real.' Rather like Mike Ross of Jessie Rae's BBQ.

The problem was that all the other writing for this book was complete, and I was caught in the middle of projects and was having a "damned" hard time getting the time to do *this* chapter.

I had researched a lot of gun stores in our area (Las Vegas / Henderson / North Las Vegas etc.) and used Google and Yelp to get a feel for the reviews about the support staff. I didn't want a big chain store type of contact. I needed down in the details about how a professional might take Joshua's challenge and solve it and therefore wanted real heavy-duty gun people.

I chose Spurlock's based on the reviews on the internet, after checking out their website.

So, I'm hours away from holding up the editing and the book is going to get behind if I don't go find a consultant FAST. I have about two hours or a touch more before Spurlock's close and I need to drive the forty-five minutes to Henderson from my place on the Strip. I choose a bad route (no thanks to you, Google Maps) and bad Vegas traffic, but I still get there fairly fast with time to spare.

When I walk in, the store is exactly what I was looking for, which is to say completely focused on guns (of all types), and I felt confident that someone in the store would have a clue about my questions...

If they didn't think I was a nutjob. I wish I had completely thought this part through and practiced how to introduce myself in the car on the way over to Spurlock's.

I came in with a laptop bag, two books (both *Torn Asunder* and *Death Becomes Her* in print) as my bona fides to prove I really was an author.

Now, I know how well my books sell, but 99.99% of America (or even greater) has NO clue who I am, so I'm very nervous when I ask to speak to someone with very specific technical questions. The person behind the counter on the left waved to the other counter (they are in an 'L' shape) and told me to speak to 'the bald one.'

I looked at him funny, since I have noticed all the guys are bald, or close to it. Fortunately, John stepped aside and waved a hand to let me know that *he* was the bald guy I needed to speak with.

I stuttered and stammered my questions out (not because I typically stutter, but because I'm nervous as hell) and started my pitch about being an author, and I have this book coming out where one of the characters needs some advice...

It wasn't going down very well.

You know that moment when you look into the eyes of the person you are speaking with and you can see them tagging you as something less than awesome? Yes, that was my feeling.

To be *TOTALLY* fair to John, here is this guy walking in off the street. I am asking very pointed questions with no context, and inadvertently took him away from a sales relationship (another counter rep was supporting the young lady and her mother) and he is now speaking to an older white guy with a black t-shirt and blue jeans claiming he is an *author* and not looking like he will buy anything.

(My wife wants to shoot, so I wouldn't be surprised if we purchase something – but I'm not going to offer that as a possibility unless it is a more solid chance than I think it was at the time.)

On top of this, I came in carrying books like I'm on a religious door-to-door proselytizing yahoo and wanting to convert him to the Church of the Damned. That he didn't kindly wave me off and escort me with a gentle (but firm) hand to my back until I was out the door was a blessing.

The further my speech went, the more relevant and intelligent questions he heard, proving I wasn't totally ignorant. His first question had to do with why I didn't just look this information up on the Internet.

A very good question, actually. The short answer was, I could have, but all that would have done was give me facts, not the wisdom to know what to do with the data. I have shot guns, but very rarely in my life. At fifty, I don't believe I have shot more than seven times in my whole life.

(I did try to shoot fish in a small stream with a .22 … Hitting those sonsabitches was *impossible*.)

Further, once I explained the issue with the metal, and my proposed solution (just spraying the metal onto the outer sides of the bullet) he was quickly able to point out the mistake in that idea.

Score one for the author!

I know when asking an expert is the right thing to do. (I am fully cognizant of my ignorance in this area. After writing over thirty books myself, I'm also cognizant that one needs to add talking about guns to sex, religion, politics, and chili as subjects that can garner very annoyed fans if you get something wrong.)

Then, John went onto explain hydroshock and the relevance of hollow-points. He effectively provided the professional advice I needed in five minutes, and then further explained the medical reasons for the justification of hydroshock theory (I later found out some do not hold to the theory) and why hollow-points are used by police (John is or was a policeman. I have a request in to find out as I've forgotten that detail.)

Then, John was kind enough to edit chapter seventeen for *accuracy*. *DAMN!* That was amazing, and I really appreciate his support of that crazy author who just showed up unannounced. I was trying to be very respectful.

I just didn't realize how crazy I must have seemed from his vantage point.

Fans are happy!

DAMN (or is this DAMNED?), this set of stories has blown WAY up, and while we are appreciative, I think I can admit that our mouths are open in surprise as well. Although my Kurtherian Gambit series took off, it didn't do this well in the first month.

One of the reasons I happen to enjoy this series is,

when you take a look at Pandora, she is the most open-minded, non-racially prejudiced, non-biased entity in the book.

I mean, she doesn't care if you are black or white, gay or straight, religious or not...she is willing to hate everyone and take advantage of each person equally and generously.

Well, she might not be pleased with incredibly hot gay guys, but that's more to do with her chances of (not) getting something from them rather than anything else, and that hurts her ego. In her opinion, she is sure that if she had the right opportunity (torture comes to mind in Hell) she would be able to get them to at least fake it with her. One of the most liberating aspects of writing this series is that Pandora can say just about anything. She's a demon. She just points out the hypocrisy of humanity from time to time. Most of us readers (should) understand that just because she says something, it doesn't de facto make it *true*.

She's a demon. Look up the word 'self-centered' in Wikipedia and it should have her picture by it.

But—and here is the piece that is unraveling as we go forward—what is going to happen with her? Pandora is 'stuck' in Katie for the time being. Katie isn't (so far) giving in to all of Pandora's requests. This is requiring more understanding of a human's opinions and ways than Pandora has had to deal with in the past, and would that change Pandora's mindset?

Plus, add to the above we have her asshole of a brother involved.

Will she go "good," and what does she know about

Heaven? She has mentioned in this book a situation a *LOOOONG* time ago that brought the Holy host down and "it wasn't pretty." I've had fans ask about angels and the short answer is, "yes, angels exist." We haven't seen any, and I can't tell you why that is.

In the next story, we start a new arc. This first four books had an arc (internally, for me) called 'Who is she now?' My purpose was to figure out this symbiotic relationship between Katie and Pandora. While I don't know what it is exactly, I have a better grasp on who they are together.

And what they *aren't*.

As we read through the next arc, we will see the team(s) start to deal with bigger issues. They will have to start working with the government, because the stakes are going to get higher.

We never know who will make it, and who won't.

We lost Armani and Garrett, and received Eric and Jeremy. Then we lost Jeremy, and received Stephanie. That was in four books. If you keep reading, we will keep writing for you. Unfortunately, unlike the Kurtherian Gambit, more characters die (or have successful exorcisms and leave us) in this series than over in that one, for good reasons.

With our second arc starting, I guess that is the question I wonder about and we will be discussing in Book Eight when we finish this next arc.

Who will still be with us?

The only ones I promise will still be here are Katie and Pandora, for without them we have no core series (and I'm not the type to kill the main characters... Well, anymore.

I've learned that lesson.) I don't plan deaths out. In fact, all I have at the moment is a general concept of what needs to occur with the team in four books, and the major change-up that sets up Katie and Pandora for Book Nine.

More cool stuff is coming. More relationships with the government. Katie is going to New York for a trip (or two) and we have a new DAMNED relationship with a new demon coming on board thanks to T'Chezz in Book Five, *Welcome To The Jungle.* (scheduled for launch April 13, 2018)

Speaking of that rat bastard T'Chezz, there is a phrase Katie says in Book Five in the beginning that I particularly like and will share here (this comes from the beats for the next story.)

Katie is still bitching about her car. "I hope my license plate's numbers," she grumps, "are imprinted on his balls..."

Sometimes, I just feel like I know exactly what Katie would say.

And it feels so DAMNED good to say it!

Ad Aeternitatem,

Michael

WRITTEN APRIL 1, 2018

Firstly, thanks so much for picking up a copy of this book. If you're still in the series with us, I'm guessing you're hankering for a Pandora bobble-head of your own, or at least craving chicken nuggets. Either way, you're our peeps. Obviously.

This last week has been a Seven Sons week for me. We just wrapped up editing for book 1 in our first series, The Immortal Huntress. It was quite a ride. I laughed, cried and got excited about where the story is going.

Seven Sons is mine and Mike's project for this summer. We're going to keep writing the hell out of Protected by the Damned, but we're doing a multi-author, multi-dimensional world called, "Seven Sons."

We have friends of ours (writers) that are taking on the lead co-author role along side us to breath life into all seven of the pure blood races that were created at the beginning of time. Mike and I spent *days* building this world and the characters. It's beautiful and has the capacity to grow into a multi-verse where lots of authors can get their feet wet in this indie world with us.

First up were the hunters. They were humans that eventually got pulled into the church in the first century AD as protectors against all evil. Where the task is quite serious, the way Kelly Hall, our Huntress co-writer goes about it is adventurous and filled with humor.

Excerpt for us from book 1: (Rebekah is our heroine)

"The academy has got our cook on a specific menu and they've cut back on her supply budget which isn't terrible, and it sure puts Lulu in a bad mood."

"Lulu is the cook?" Rebekah hoped she'd be able to remember everyone's names.

"Yes. Laura Pembroke. She's a strong personality, so making her upset, well, I don't know quite how to put it, but let's just say you either love her or hate her, and vice versa."

"I like her already," came a voice only steps away. Ignis approached with his hands in his pockets and looking a lot more relaxed with his suit coat missing and his shirt collar undone. He'd even rolled up his sleeves as if he would ever attempt manual labor. He noticed Rebekah looking and pushed one of his sleeves up higher. "Let's meet her, shall we?"

Sister Frankie tensed as she opened the door to the kitchen in time to hear a crash. "Son-of-a-biscuit-eating-mother," came a voice from across the room.

Sister Frankie leaned in close to Rebekah and Ignis and shielded her mouth to whisper, "She's really suffering with the loss."

"Obviously," said Ignis under his breath as he and Rebekah exchanged a look.

They continued in behind the sister who stopped before getting too close. "Lulu, I have someone I'd like you to meet?"

The tiny woman stuck her head up from behind the counter. "Well, that's just great," mumbled Lulu causing the sister to grow red with blush as she tucked as loose hair into her veil.

The old woman stood and once righted she squared her shoulders and curled her lip at the sight of them. "Who's this and can they get me a decent oven mitt?" The older woman's attitude was at least three feet taller than she was.

"This is Rebekah Ward, and Ignis—I'm sorry I didn't catch your last name." Sister Frankie gave him an apologetic look.

"I'm kind of a one-name wonder." Ignis only used his last name when legally necessary.

"Who is this guy, some kind of boy band reject? Ginger Slice?" Lulu wiped her hands on her apron and extended a hand to Rebekah, who promptly took it and gave her a smile.

"No, ma'am. This one can't carry a tune to save his life." She turned her eyes to her friend whose face was now as red as his hair.

Ha! I love that scene. Little does Kelly know, I was named Lulu when I was a little girl. I could easily match the attitude of this cook on a good, hot Texas summer day.

In other news, I owe you that eternally stupid Christmas cookies video. It's something my personal assistant put together alongside my daughter, who's trying to bring me and hubs into the next wave of social media. Video.

"I'm a writer. Why do I have to bake cookies online with my brother (who I co-write with) as if we do this shit all the time? It's a lie?!?" Me… throwing a fit over this absurdity.

"Because, Mother. (I only get called "mother" when I'm being unreasonable. Like 99% of the time with my oldest daughter.) Your readers want to see you living life. (Lies) And this will be cute!"

"Excellent. Cute." I give a 'kill me now' look and move into cute mode with my little brother who is much more compliant than I.

So here is the cookie making video. The damn things tasted like salt rocks when they were done because I wasn't really paying attention to the cookies. I was trying to be entertaining. Good luck with that. So now I look like I can't cook. Hey! Maybe that's a good thing. LOL!

Enjoy the video or roll your eyes and move on about your day grateful that you're not a puppet to a millennial social media managing kid. And after that, enjoy some more great stories.

We do what we do for you, but I'm thinking you knew that.

Slave to many stories,

Laurie Starkey

ENTER THE KURTHERIAN GAMBIT UNIVERSE

Available At Amazon

CONNECT WITH MICHAEL TODD

Want more?

Find us On Facebook

https://www.facebook.com/Protected-by-the-Damned-193345908061855/

KURTHERIAN GAMBIT SERIES TITLES INCLUDE:

FIRST ARC

Death Becomes Her (01) - Queen Bitch (02) - Love Lost (03) -
Bite This (04) - Never Forsaken (05) - Under My Heel (06) -
Kneel Or Die (07)

SECOND ARC

We Will Build (08) - It's Hell To Choose (09) -
Release The Dogs of War (10) - Sued For Peace (11) -
We Have Contact (12) - My Ride is a Bitch (13) -
Don't Cross This Line (14)

THIRD ARC

Never Submit (15) - Never Surrender (16) - Forever Defend (17)
Might Makes Right (18) - Ahead Full (19) - Capture Death (20) -
Life Goes On (21)

THE SECOND DARK AGES
* with Ell Leigh Clarke *

The Dark Messiah (01) - The Darkest Night (02) -
Darkest Before The Dawn (03) - Dawn Arrives (04)

THE BORIS CHRONICLES
* with Paul C. Middleton *
Evacuation (1) - Retaliation (2) - Revelations (3) -
Redemption (04)

RECLAIMING HONOR
* with Justin Sloan *
Justice Is Calling (01) - Claimed By Honor (02) -
Judgement Has Fallen (03) - Angel of Reckoning (04) -
Born Into Flames (05) - Defending The Lost (06) -
Saved By Valor (07) - Return of Victory (08)

THE ETHERIC ACADEMY
* with TS Paul *
ALPHA CLASS (01) - ALPHA CLASS - Engineering (02)

TERRY HENRY "TH" WALTON CHRONICLES
* with Craig Martelle *
Nomad Found (01) - Nomad Redeemed (02) -
Nomad Unleashed (03) - Nomad Supreme (04) -
Nomad's Fury (05) - Nomad's Justice (06) -
Nomad Avenged (07) - Nomad Mortis (08) - Nomad's Force (09)
Nomad's Galaxy (10)

TRIALS AND TRIBULATIONS
* with Natalie Grey *
Risk Be Damned (01) - Damned to Hell (02)

A NEW DAWN

* with Amy Hopkins *

Dawn of Destiny (01) - Dawn of Darkness (02) -
Dawn of Deliverance (03) - Dawn of Days (04)

TALES OF THE WELLSPRING KNIGHT

* with P.J. Cherubino *

Knight's Creed (01) - Knight's Struggle (02)

~THE AGE OF MADNESS~

LIVE FREE OR DIE

with Haley Lawson

Unleashing Madness (01)

~THE AGE OF EXPANSION~

THE ASCENSION MYTH

* with Ell Leigh Clarke *

Awakened (01) - Activated (02) - Called (03) - Sanctioned (04) -
Rebirth (05) - Retribution (06) - Cloaked (07) -
Bourne (08)

CONFESSIONS OF A SPACE ANTHROPOLOGIST

* with Ell Leigh Clarke *

Giles Kurns: Rogue Operator (01)
Giles Kurns: Rogue Instigator (02)

THE UPRISE SAGE

* with Amy Duboff *

Covert Talents (01) - Endless Advance (02) - Veiled Designs (03) - Dark Rivals (04)

BAD COMPANY

* with Craig Martelle *

The Bad Company (01) - Blockade (02) - Price of Freedom (03)

THE GHOST SQUADRON

* with Sarah Noffke *

Formation (01) - Exploration (02) - Evolution (03) - Degeneration (04) - Impersonation (05)

VALERIE'S ELITES

* with Justin Sloan and PT Hylton *

Valerie's Elites (01) - Death Defied (02) - Prime Enforcer (03)

SHADOW VANGUARD

with Tom Dublin

Gravity Storm (01)

ETHERIC ADVENTURES: ANNE AND JINX

* with S.R. Russell *

Etheric Recruit (01) - Etheric Researcher (02)

www.ingramcontent.com/pod-product-compliance
Lightning Source LLC
Chambersburg PA
CBHW022024120726
47898CB00007BA/2114